CHRISTIAN HAYES is the author of *The Glass Book*, *The Fat Detective*, *The Fat Detective in Love* and *The Fat Detective Disappears*. He lives and writes in London.

CHRISTIAN HAYES

The Fat Detective

The Fat Detective

The Following Is Not Based on a True Story

1997

Chapter A

My bones were a mess. Imagine a fat man - a really fat man - covered from head to toe in plaster with two sad little eyes peering out. There was so much glueing me together that I had become encased in my very own shell and the pain of my cracked bones meant that I was on all kinds of painkillers, resulting in a soupy brain and unintelligible speech. Words slurred so badly that they lost all meaning and I found it far easier to just say nothing at all.

So here I was, this fat, mute, mummified man, rising and falling from sleep with no sense of night or day. To make it worse my neck was in a brace so I could only stare straight ahead. Luckily a TV was bolted to the wall ahead of me but a missing remote meant that it only beamed out old movies where men wore overcoats and women sparkled. My days became a pleasant blend of dreams and movies interrupted only by shocking chords of pain that crashed through my body.

In *How Lonely Was My Grave* (RKO, 1942) a desperate detective with a bullet lodged in his body makes his way to his office where he collapses in the shadows, sweat pouring off his forehead. As he bleeds to death the silhouette of a *femme fatale* appears behind the frosted glass where the name of the detective agency is embossed backwards (yellaM'O & yellaM'O). The pistol was in her fist when it fired that bullet in the previous scene but it wasn't clear whether he or her gangster husband was the intended target. I never got to find out what happened though because Nurse Banerjee, a *femme fatale* in her own quiet way, used her hefty frame to effortlessly block the TV.

'I've got a surprise for you,' she said. She always raised her voice when she spoke to me as though I was ninety. 'Your wife is here to see you. You never told me how *beautiful* she is.'

That was all very well but there was only one problem. I wasn't married. Needless to say I was far more surprised than the nurse could have imagined.

And the *femme fatale* who stepped into my line of sight certainly was beautiful. A dark green herringbone coat outlined her body and a scarlet cloche hat covered her deep red hair. But her beauty had long since faded for me. Instead it was fear that shot through me the instant I saw her. And after all I knew about her she still looked like a delicate thing, like a china doll that would break if touched. I squirmed within my shell but it only brought me pain.

'Eugene,' said Melissa. Her eyes were already filled with crocodile tears by the time she sat down and placed her hand on my plastered arm. 'Oh, look at you, just *look* at you. I really didn't mean for anything like this to happen. I haven't been able to *live* with myself. I knew I had to come down here to see you.' She quietened for a moment before springing it on me: 'I'm going away. But I want you to promise me one thing, that you won't try and find me. Please promise me. It just won't do either of us any good. But before I left I just wanted to come down here and explain myself. How it all started and how it came to this. I just need you to know that I'm not a bad person, really I'm not.' She continued to talk but I already understood that it was nobody's fault but my own. It was a stupid decision, made only a few weeks earlier, that got me into this mess.

Chapter B

I clicked it into existence and suddenly it was official. Amid requests for second-hand bicycles and first-hand piano lessons, it looked distinctly out of place.

Private Detective For Hire. No Case Too Small.

Contact Eugene H. Blake at
eugenehblake@hotmail.com

The problem was that I wasn't a private detective. I was an accountant. And I didn't know anything about being a private detective. But I was a desperate man and a kind of madness had seeped into my bones. A more sane person would have suggested an easier solution to my problems. A holiday, perhaps, or a brisk walk in the countryside. No. I concluded that the only solution to my problems was to become a private dick.

The idea crept into my brain on the London Underground, on that stretch of Central Line that yo-yoed me back and forth throughout the city every day. Ten times a week. Four hundred and fifty-six times a year. Please mind the gap between the train and the platform. This is a Central line train to Hainault via

Newbury Park. Not to mention that walk from my flat to the Broadway, those same endless stretches of pavement: over the roundabout, left at the school, across the green. And it was on those infuriating commutes, pressed against the bodies of strangers, that I started to fantasise about a different life altogether.

Back in my university days a member of my halls of residence dropped out of his course and moved back home. Just before he left I received a knock at the door.

'You want these?' he asked. At his feet was a box filled with books. 'Too heavy,' he said. His name was Peterson but that doesn't really matter.

'Sure,' I said, dragging that box into my room and shutting the door. I didn't really care either way but in those student days I never passed up anything I could get for free.

And one Saturday night, when all the other students had found parties to go to, I pulled one out of the box. *The Electric Detective* by Henry Silverling, it was called. I didn't usually read these kinds of books but after reading a line ('When the blue smoke of his cigarette parted, Jack Claw saw a brunette standing barefoot on the ledge of the Brooklyn Bridge.') I was hooked. I read the whole thing in one sitting and it was morning when I finally closed that tatty paperback. And one book led to another. *The Iron Fedora*, *Trigger Finger* and *Whiskey Boulevard*. I found them more educational than my Applied Economics lectures so I skipped classes in favour of page-turning those quickie crime novels. I locked myself in my room with a supply of crisps, cokes and custard creams and didn't leave for days on end.

All these years later I had almost forgotten about that

box of books but on that tube, as a man sneezed in my vicinity, I spotted a commuter with a copy of *The Electric Detective* in her hands. It brought it all back to me and in memory it felt like it was someone else entirely who had read them. And it brought back some long-forgotten fantasies, the fantasy of being a private detective and the thought that adventure was written into my future. Well that future was already passing me by and I found that I had no time to do anything. Working nine to six meant that I barely saw the sun and when I got home I would collapse with exhaustion but they just kept paying me so I just kept showing up.

Sitting at my desk, this fantasy started to turn as concrete as the car park outside my office window. I thought about it to the point where I started to believe I actually *was* a private detective. And this thought, this wild fantasy, became a lifeline, a parachute for my soul. It felt like the only thing that was going to save me from the ravaging apathy that had invaded my life.

And that's what led to me sitting at my computer screen that night, staring at that blinking cursor and my hastily-composed advertisement. The London skyline was craning its neck to take a look at me through the window. It saw a man who had to wear braces because they don't make belts long enough, holding up trousers ordered from a catalogue for the big and tall. And I'm not even that tall.

In my screen's reflection I looked at my permanently knotted brow and into my desperate eyes and then it came, like it always did, the blotches of red, one by one, each one staining my white office shirt. I grabbed my nose and hurried to the bathroom. In childhood there was the look-up method to stop the flow but that was superseded by the look-down method somewhere along the way. I watched the steady drip glow red on the shining porcelain, then at my face in the mirror, with its single streak of red from my lip to my chin.

Chapter C

The doctor stared at me, her desk cluttered with paper, as she pushed her glasses up her nose. She didn't blink.

'It's been happening more and more,' I explained, my face still red from the flight of stairs outside the surgery. 'Two to three times a week, I'd say. The first time it happened I was in a meeting.'

'I wouldn't worry about it,' the doctor said. Even though she was staring right at me, she was distracted. She turned to her computer screen. 'You were here last week, yes? For the…'

'For the itch.'

'And how's that going?'

'I'm using the cream and it's kind of been working, but it's at night when…'

'If you could just pull up your sleeve,' she said, interrupting me.

She slapped a velcro armband around my forearm and set it expanding, gripping me painfully, as the numbers on the blood pressure reader ticked ever-higher.

'When was the last time you had a check-up?'

'A check-up? I couldn't say.'

She looked at the results. 'Hmmm. And if you could

open your shirt for me, please.'

She pressed the cold circle of stethoscope against my chest. 'Breathe in…' I did so. 'And breathe out…'

Soon enough I was being weighed. I hadn't been on a weighing scale since I was fifteen and had dodged them ever since. I was shocked by the violence applied to that needle, a sharp leap to the right.

At least she didn't make me take my trousers off.

'About these nosebleeds…' I said as I sat down.

'I wouldn't worry about them. You're probably just a little depressed, that's all.'

'Oh, I see. Is that bad?'

'I'm more worried about your weight. For your height it puts you in the category of…' She checked her chart… 'Morbidly obese.'

'*Morbidly obese*?' If I was a little depressed when I came in I was going to be suicidal by the time I left.

'You're going to have to make some drastic changes to your lifestyle.'

'You mean like take a holiday?'

'Do you ever exercise?'

'When do I have time for it? I get up, trudge to work, sit at my desk all day, scoff a sandwich, trudge home, sleep badly and then start the process again. When is there time for exercise?'

'Before work. You could go for a swim.'

'I'm not really a morning person.'

'The evening then.'

'Why work if you can't enjoy the evening?' I didn't mention that all I did was eat and pass out.

'When men are in their forties they have to understand—'

'I'm not in my forties!'

'Oh, you just look…' She checked the file again. 'Ah yes, you're right. Well you can't keep this up much longer. Your diet is going to have to change.' Perhaps I shouldn't tell her that the whole time I was in there I was thinking about the patisserie I had spotted across the road. Breakfast had been over an hour ago and, well, I'm only human.

Chapter D

The doctor had made me so depressed about my weight that I immediately bought a cream horn and chocolate eclair to cheer me up. And as I filled my chops with those creamy dreams everything felt okay again. I knew that they didn't count towards that new regime that the doctor had been talking about but I just needed a treat to inspire me. And as I pushed that eclair into my mouth I spotted something in the charity shop window across the street. An old department store mannequin was wearing something that I straight away took as a sign: a 1940s raincoat.

Somehow the buttons met the buttonholes and the fabric belt buckled with even a hole to spare. I looked at myself in the mirror and I was no longer Eugene H. Blake. The man who looked back at me was someone else entirely, a private detective with a slew of cases already under his belt. He and his raincoat were already embroiled in a life of mystery and adventure. There was history in that coat.

'A lovely coat that is,' said the wiry man when I stepped up to buy it. 'Almost sold it this morning. Must be your lucky day.'

'Maybe it is.' I paid up and headed out into the rain.

As I left I saw the man outfitting the naked mannequin with my old coat.

Let me explain what it feels like to be in a body like mine. If you were to walk from here to the end of the street, by the time you passed that postbox you would be out of breath. Your back hurts and your legs ache from keeping up all this weight. You start to cheat, to find any way out of walking that you can: hopping on buses, taking tubes, paying for taxis, or just not going out at all. You stay in all weekend so that you don't have to face the struggle of walking.

I found it strange, then, that this raincoat gave me the ability to walk further than I ever had been able to before. It started the moment I walked out of that charity shop, my hours circling the streets. That coat somehow gave me more energy and even made me more observant than I had ever been before. Instead of staring at the cracks in the pavement I now looked up and saw details in the buildings I had passed a million times before. I started to see animals and angels and monograms carved out in the stone. And I started to look into the faces of those strangers passing me by, all those men and women who drift through the city, and I realised that they did not see me at all. None of them returned the gaze offered to them, each locked in their own troubled world. William Blake was right about those marks of weakness, marks of woe. That hadn't changed in two hundred years.

I stopped walking and looked down at my feet, encased in decade-old spongy white trainers. It really didn't do anything for my new life as a private eye so I marched into the nearest shoe shop and walked out with some proper leather shoes - you know, the kind that grown-ups wear, with laces and everything - and promptly shoved my tatty Reeboks into the nearest bin. And now I could really feel the city beneath my feet as my leather soles kissed the pavement.

While London by day is as grey as its miles of pavement, by night it takes on a character that is closer to mysterious than beautiful. That night the whole city was slick with rain, its inky black landscape dotted with the colourful reflections of headlights, street lamps and electric signs. And when it started to rain I was prepared. I just turned the collar up on my raincoat and kept marching on. I felt like I was disappearing and that I could go forever.

The raincoat appeared to hold special properties. Not only could I walk for hours through the rain, it also transformed the people around me. Where I had previously seen innocent strangers I now saw characters up to no good. A man in thick-rimmed glasses sitting in the back row of a cinema became a fugitive from justice, hiding out in the darkness from the arm of the law. A tired cafe owner's dreary surroundings hid a past strewn with dark secrets. No one knew of his past life as an amateur boxer and anyone who tried to mess with him would get a mean hook to the jaw. A businesswoman waiting at a bus stop was in fact a spy with a microfilm hidden in the sole of her shoe and a loaded pistol strapped inside her black winter coat.

The city took on a sinister feel, transformed itself into a world of intrigue, mystery and suspicion.

It was late when I returned to my local high street, a high street I knew so well that I never gave it very much thought at all. A pharmacy, a newsagent's, a butcher's, a hardware store and two kebab shops, one at each end. I would make the extra effort to walk to West Kebab at the end of the high street. They were masters, absolute artists of the doner kebab with inventions so imaginative they should have been handed awards. Their Mixed Kebab had a big brother called The Special. Not only did it mix chicken, lamb and doner, but it was also covered in chips and melted cheese. I had come to know the three brothers in there quite well. Their father helped out on weekends; a real family business.

'Matey,' he'd call me, since he didn't know my name and I didn't know his, 'where have you been?'

'I've been busy.'

'You haven't been going to South Ealing for your kebabs again, have you?' He looked genuinely concerned.

'I've learned from my mistakes.'

'Because we make the best kebabs in London, you know. There's no need to go anywhere else.'

'This I know.'

'How you been keeping?'

'Not good,' I said.

'Whatever it is it's nothing a Special can't fix.'

'Give me your very best.'

'Coming right up and for you I'll make it extra special - I'll throw in a Fanta for free. Take it from the fridge and don't tell the other customers.'

This artisan of the kebab deftly danced around the ingredients, delicately sprinkling red lettuce, green lettuce, red onion, chicken doner, lamb doner, chilli sauce, garlic sauce, cheese and chips. All wrapped up in one beautiful greasy package.

'I hope you're hungry.'

This thing was so huge I had to support it with both hands. I took it to one of the rickety tables in the corner and sunk into it. I didn't know if I was eating it or it was eating me. Either way it seemed to make everything okay.

The night everything changed I was sitting at my computer, listening to the mystical wailings of my 56k modem as it dialled up and launched me onto the information super highway. My only companion was a giant pizza wheel that had been delivered by a Bengali motorcyclist moments earlier. He had kindly added eight chicken wings, a two-litre bottle of coke and a tub of vanilla ice cream to the order, not to mention an entire second pizza.

There really is no greater pleasure in this world than eating pizza alone. There is a purity to the task ahead of you, to the task of finishing each slice, each one an achievement in itself that brings you closer to your goal. Pizza can really make life simple.

'You've got mail,' said the polite voice to me as a smattering of junk mail flooded my inbox. Offers for gold watches, viagra pills and an email that threatened bad luck if I didn't pass it on. But in amongst them was a reply. It was simple and all it said was:

Services required. Tomorrow, 8pm, 89 Princes Gardens.

* * *

My eyes stared up at the ceiling as that blue morning light crept back into my room. It wasn't the question of whether I would take up the offer or not that kept me awake. That was decided almost without any thought at all. Instead I thought about myself and realised I was no longer who I once was. Almost with a sense of regret I could feel Eugene Blake becoming a little fictional.

Chapter E

It was seven thirty in the evening by the time I made it to Ealing Broadway but instead of taking the Central Line as I had every morning for the last eleven years I took the District Line, that notoriously incompetent branch of the Underground. I had to wait for ten minutes for a train to show up and then another ten for it to actually leave. 'This train is for all stations to Upminster,' the driver announced as the train groaned into motion, struggling to push its own weight along the tracks. Something I could certainly relate to. Across the station the Central Line tube just sped off into the distance and disappeared.

I rode the trundling carriage only a couple of stops and got off at Acton Town.

As I exited the station I fished out the address from my raincoat pocket and headed into the drizzling darkness of the evening. Turning onto Princes Gardens I was confronted by a face I would later come to know very well. On the corner a poster was pinned to the trunk of a tree. 'David White. Missing. Last seen 23rd October.' And I found the same poster on the next tree, and the next, until I realised that every single tree on the street was pinned with the image of David White as though he were a lost dog.

Looking up from the address in my hand I found, obscured by tall hedges, a pristine little mansion. I let myself into the swinging gate and walked through the neat little front garden dotted with complicated flowers. A thick ring was hanging out of a brass lion's jaws. I knocked it firmly but after silence I noticed a doorbell. Bing bong.

The intercom crackled and threw a couple of words at me: 'You're *late*.' I checked my Casio. Nine minutes, yes. A buzz and I pushed the door to find a dim, square hallway. A painting of an English lake in an ornate gold frame dominated the little space.

A voice called down from somewhere beyond the stairs.

'Wait in the living room.'

An entirely white room: white fireplace, white sofa, white coffee table. I snooped, my eyes scanning the bookshelves. Classic novels in serious hardback editions sat alongside colourful beach reads in no particular order. Large-format books on photography and fashion mingled with cookbooks on Indian, Mediterranean and Italian food. One shelf was lined solely with the yellow spines of National Geographic.

Every surface around the room was clear. Nothing sat on the coffee table, nothing on the dining table. The floor was clear of shoes, of bags. You could photograph it for a magazine spread without having to change a thing.

Melissa White, framed in the doorway, took all the air out of the room. In that slice of time, only a few heartbeats long, she seemed like the most exquisite creature I had ever seen. Long auburn hair, deep green eyes, full pink lips. Her hair was damp and her body filled the air with the fresh scents of a hot bath. Her impeccable clothes hung lightly to her and made no secret of the curves underneath.

'Eugene Blake,' was all I could think to say and held out my hand. She looked me up and down, clearly puzzled by the colossal man taking up space in her living room. She squeezed my fingers with her soft left hand. Her right was holding a cigarette.

'Melissa…' she said, blowing out a lungful of blue smoke. 'White'.

She draped her body on the sofa, slid her slippers off and rested her bare feet on a cushion. From there she had another look.

'Help yourself to a drink. Behind you.'

Amidst the assortment of whiskies and vodkas in the drinks cabinet I cracked open a can of Coke. She didn't look too impressed.

'Take a seat.' She gestured to a dainty wooden chair by the window. I perched myself on it as delicately as I could. 'It's an antique,' she said. I could feel it creaking under me.

'You will find him, won't you?' Those emerald eyes gleamed up at me through a fresh cloud of smoke. 'He should have been home by now. I've made him dinner every night for his return. I keep expecting him just to walk through the door. Even just now, when you rang the bell, I thought for a split second that it could have been David and he was just returning home as though nothing had ever happened. Not that I'm not *thrilled* to meet you.'

'When did he go missing?'

'October twenty-third,' she said quickly, as though

she had repeated it many times over already. 'He went to work one Monday morning three weeks ago and never returned.'

'Where does he work?'

'He's an audiologist and has worked all around the world but he was at Ealing Hospital. He was on the verge of moving somewhere more prestigious.'

'Did he show up at the hospital that Monday morning?'

'Yes. He saw a few patients in the morning, chatted with colleagues, but by the time lunchtime came around he had vanished.'

'When was the last time you heard from him? Did you speak to him that day?' She seemed to steady herself a little.

'I said goodbye to him that morning. I was brushing my teeth and he called from the hallway that he'd be late. It was such an insignificant event that I'm almost embarrassed to say that I can hardly remember it.'

'And when did you first realise he had disappeared?'

'The next morning.'

'You didn't find it strange that he didn't come home that night?'

She ignored the question and sat up, slipping her feet and all their painted toes back into her slippers.

'How much do you charge for this sort of thing anyway?' Until that moment I hadn't really thought about it. Even so I came up with something.

'One hundred a day plus expenses.' I had no idea where that came from.

'Expenses?'

'You know, transportation, lunch.'

'How about one hundred pounds and no expenses?'

'Fine,' I said. I wasn't one to argue.

She leaned in a little. 'How are you going to find him? How do you go about finding someone?'

I didn't really know how to answer because I hadn't yet given it any thought.

'It's like when you lose anything, really. You think about where you were when you last saw it, retrace your steps. One time I lost my glasses, I was looking all over for them, and they were on my head the whole time.' I don't wear glasses.

'My husband is not a pair of glasses, Mr. Blake.'

'I know but what I'm saying is…' That chair was really creaking under me now.

'What are you saying?'

I gulped some Coke out of the can. 'That, you know, you have to put yourself in their position. Therefore I will put myself in your husband's shoes. I want to think how he thinks.' I also had no idea where this was coming from. 'If someone disappears, it's for a reason. Your husband either disappeared willingly or unwillingly and if I can find the motivation for disappearing I have a much greater chance of finding out where he's ended up.'

'I can tell you now, Mr. Blake, that my husband did not disappear willingly.' The air grew frosty and she dragged sharply on that cigarette, her eyes drifting towards the darkness that pressed up against the French doors.

'You said he didn't come home the night he disappeared. How come you weren't concerned then? How come it only took until the following morning to discover he was missing?'

Her eyes fixed on me.

'Look,' she said, as if she was debating with herself whether to say anything at all, 'I wasn't concerned that night because my husband and I... let's just say we sleep in separate rooms.'

'I see. And you expected him to be out late?'

'Some nights he went out late, yes, and would return long after I was asleep.'

'Do you know where your husband went on these nights out?'

'My husband wasn't well. He had a kind of insomnia. Sometimes he'd go take a walk just to clear his head and he wouldn't return until the next morning.'

'Where had he been?'

'Your guess is as good as mine. He said he just wandered the street.'

'All night long?'

'All night long.'

'Did this happen a lot?'

'From time to time. So when he didn't come home on the twenty-third I just assumed he'd walk through the door the next morning. But morning came and there was no sign of him. I didn't know what to do so I called the police.'

'And what did they say?'

'They sent me to the Missing Persons Bureau. I gave them his details and a photo and they sent me boxes of posters. I've been putting them up ever since.'

'Where did you think he actually went on those nights?'

'Like I told you, he said he just walked the streets.'

'And you believed him?'

'Look, I'm not stupid. I know how the world works. But I want you to promise me that if you ever find out there was anyone *else*, keep it from me. I want to go to my grave with the David I knew preserved in memory.'

'Why don't you think he hasn't called? To at least let you know he's okay?'

'He wasn't thinking straight.'

'Not thinking straight?'

'I am going to trust your code of silence, or whatever you call it. What I am about to tell you is not to leave these four walls.'

'My lips are sealed,' I said. I didn't know what code she was talking about.

'This is something I haven't told anyone before and David kept this secret locked inside of him. In private he suffered from a very disturbing form of depression. He seemed perfectly normal, would go to work, do his job, act as though everything was okay. He would smile and crack jokes and you'd never know it was there deep down beneath the surface. But I was the one who saw it up close: the desperation and sleeplessness. He saw a doctor a few weeks ago and got started on a new regime of medication. Initially it helped him but the effects quickly wore off and just before he disappeared he had stopped taking his medication completely.

'When I knew the police wouldn't be able to help I looked for someone who could. And then I found your ad. He confided in me the thoughts he was having. These were deep, dark, disturbing thoughts, the worst kind of thoughts you could have. They've scarred me and I can't stop turning them around in my brain. We don't have much time and I'm terrified I will never see him again. Every minute not looking for him is a minute not saving him. And that is why you have to help me, Mr. Blake. That is why you have to find my husband. It is a matter of life and death.'

When I placed the ad I thought I'd end up looking for lost dogs but here I was, an accountant with zero sleuthing experience and a matter of life and death on my fat little hands.

Chapter F

To get my mind working it had to be the only thing that would give me the energy I required for my day ahead: the Full English Breakfast. But the secret to a great full English is that the greasier it is the better. So I went to the only place that could give me what I needed: Porky's Pantry, one of the last of the original *caffs* left in London. The O on its sign had been substituted by a pig wearing a bow tie. In the window was that same, jolly pig, this time in an apron and holding up a plate of bacon and eggs. The chalkboard on the street boasted of the delicacies inside: Bangers and Mash, Fish and Chips, Jacket Potatoes. But it was the Full English I came for. There was Porky's Super Fry Up, Porky's Country Breakfast or, for the foolish, Porky's Giant Breakfast. And sitting in one of its half-sized, two-person booths you could only but marvel at the pig memorabilia that filled the place. Pig posters, pig postcards, pig calendars. There was even a shelf covered in all kinds of piggy banks.

So I found myself in Porky's Pantry, being served up a plate of everything I could have wanted: two wobbly fried eggs, three meaty sausages, two thick rashers of bacon, a whole fried tomato, a handful of button mushrooms with two slices of fried toast on the side as well as a mug of milky coffee. I, however, had also decided to go 'the whole hog', as they called it, which increased the size of the plate and added hash browns, black pudding and a mountain of bubble and squeak. Oh, and all this swimming in an ocean of baked beans.

By the time I finished it dawned on me that this gargantuan meal had not given me the energy I had been looking for. I was exhausted, weighed down by the mass of food that was inside me. This made walking extra difficult but luckily I was only heading to the bookshop next door. I heaved myself out of the chair (I mean, first things first), complimented the chef and headed out the door.

'Do you have anything on how to be a private detective?' I asked.

The teenager punched the keys on the keyboard.

Private Eyes: A Writer's Guide to Private Investigators. Sure, it was for fiction writers but I thumbed through it anyway to see what I could find. It had been published in 1988 so not only was it out of date but it was also American, meaning that the phone numbers and services it listed were of no use. What I did find useful, however, was the list of equipment that every PI supposedly needs. A pencil, a notebook, a tape recorder, a camera, binoculars, a pocket torch, a pen knife and a fingerprint kit.

It also suggested a gun.

In the U.S. I'm sure it's easy to walk into your local friendly firearms store but in W.H. Smith guns are really hard to find. There were some other odd items that it suggested too, like a bulletproof raincoat (a mere $1,200) or a hat with a ponytail attached. Ah, the perfect disguise.

I visited the local camping gear shop, a place I had never stepped into before, and bought a compact pair of binoculars, a small metal torch and a Victorinox Swiss Army Knife. It had everything I needed on there: a corkscrew, a toothpick and a tiny magnifying glass. Now I really felt like a detective.

I called the Missing People charity and asked whether they had had any reported sightings of David White. They hadn't had any responses to his poster and by the time the conversation was over they had almost entirely convinced me that finding David White was an impossibility. Every two minutes, they informed me, someone in Britain disappears. Most of them would be found within forty-eight hours but the rest of them might never be found. There were one hundred and seventy-seven dead bodies identified in Britain last year but many more than that were left unidentified.

'We find that there are two reasons for someone to disappear,' said the voice on the phone. 'One is to start a new life and in this case they will be doing everything in their power not to be found by all the people from their old one. The other is that they're already dead and that's the reason why they're unable to make contact with anyone.' Death certainly could get in the way of getting things done. 'Every day people do really vanish into thin air.' She told me that the people who don't want to be found almost always change their appearance, either changing the colour of their hair or growing a beard.

I spent the next ten minutes drawing a biro beard on one of David's photos.

This was going to be much harder than I thought.

Chapter G

My eyes drifted from the posters for pregnancy and prostates to the miserable faces of the unwell that dotted the waiting room. After asking about the missing doctor I had to wait over two hours before someone would talk to me. Eventually the receptionist exchanged a few words about me to Dr. Charlotte Bell who had been popping up and disappearing all morning. This doctor approached me.

'Yes?'

Her too-blue eyes were the first thing I noticed. Her shimmering blonde hair was the second.

'I'm here about David White.' She took a second to look me up and down.

'And you are?'

I patted my jacket for the I.D. I didn't have.

'My name is Blake. I'm here to investigate.'

'*Investigate?*'

'Yes.'

'Where did you get that coat? The 1940s?'

'No, Ealing.'

'There's nothing I can tell you about David that everyone doesn't already know and I've got patients booked all day so I don't really have the time...'

'Melissa sent me,' I said, interrupting her. Now she really looked me over.

'You've got two minutes. *Two*. Come with me.'

She took a bunch of keys out of her pocket, sorted through them and unlocked a door along the corridor.

'Wait inside. Don't touch anything.'

She let me in and shut the door behind me, the frosted glass rattling in its frame.

The office looked as though David had walked out moments ago rather than three weeks earlier. A jacket hung on the back of the chair and the desk was covered with papers as though David had been in the middle of his work. I examined his medical equipment: stethoscopes, tongue depressors, ear examiners. In the corner of the room I found a plastic model of the human head. I lifted the skull to reveal layers of plastic brain underneath.

I opened his desk drawers, each one stuffed full of papers. It's a wonder he could find anything. Then I checked the jacket, finding my hand dipping into the inside pocket at the very moment the door opened. I quickly closed my fist over whatever I found and stuffed it into my raincoat pocket.

'What are you doing?' asked Charlotte, her hand still clutching the door handle.

'Nothing,' I said, standing suspiciously behind the desk. She glanced over her shoulder before shutting the door and locking it from the inside.

In her hand was a large notebook which she opened out on the desk.

'These are the appointment logs from the day that David disappeared. You can see here that David had plenty of appointments; the first at eight thirty, the second at nine. He went on to see patients all the way up to twelve-thirty. But that was when it became a mystery. One of the nurses pulled me out of a consultation and told me that David could not be found, that his patients were crowding up the waiting room. When I checked his office it was exactly as it is now.'

'You saw him yourself that morning?'

'Yes.'

'What time was that?'

'About a quarter to eight.'

'And how did he seem?'

'Absolutely normal. His usual self.'

'What did you talk about?'

'It was just small talk, nothing very significant. We talked about how there weren't enough coffee filters and the patients we had lined up for the day.'

'Were you surprised when he disappeared?'

'Yes - he's a hugely kind and responsible person. He just wouldn't desert his patients like that.'

'Why do you think he left?'

'I don't know but it couldn't have been of his own free will... it's hard to explain. I mean, I've *seen* the video.'

'The video?'

'The camera at reception. On the tape you can see him walking out of his office, through the reception and out of the building. But it doesn't look in any way like he's leaving for good.'

'No?'

'He only had his shirt on, no jacket. His jacket's right here. I went out to the car park and where his car had been was just an empty space.'

'He drove away?'

'Yes. There's footage of that too.'

'Do you have any opinions about it. I mean, why do you think he disappeared like that? Did you know if he was having any problems?'

'You're not going to be able to *dig up* anything on him if that's what you're thinking. He's an excellent doctor and his patients adore him. He's always had a very thorough, methodical approach to everything he's done. He'd always go the extra mile for those in need. He is a compassionate person at heart.'

As she spoke, a redness was creeping up her neck and into her cheeks.

'Did he ever confide in anyone around here?'

'In what way?'

'Did you talk about his private life?'

'We talked. I'd say he considered me a friend.'

'Was there ever any suggestion of problems between him and Melissa?'

'There were things he told me ...but I don't feel comfortable divulging to a stranger.' She couldn't stop herself from letting out further details. I could tell she was itching to say more. 'But every marriage has their problems. His was no different.'

'Problems? Was there someone else?' I asked flatly. I tried to sneak it in there, as though she wouldn't notice the brazenness of the question. But she did notice: her eyes narrowed and she stood a little taller.

'I didn't say that.' It was clearly enough to end the conversation. She no longer wanted to reveal any more to me. 'I've given you more than enough time. I have patients waiting for me.'

'Okay, well, thank you for your time.'

'Just find him,' she said, gripping my arm. The

redness returned. 'Just find him for me.'

Chapter H

A doctor wakes up in the morning, puts on his clothes, ties his shoelaces, eats his cereal, says goodbye to his wife, gets into his car and drives off like he does on every other day of his life. But this time he doesn't go to work. Instead he passes right by the hospital where he works and keeps driving along the road, heading West. No, his colleague Dr. Charlotte Bell says she saw him in the morning. So he wakes up in the morning, ties his tie, eats his toast, says goodbye to his wife, drives to the hospital. He prepares for the day, checks his mail, has a coffee, checks his diary. He sees his first patient and then his second. To the first he looks into his ears and prescribes ear drops. To the second he tests her hearing and demonstrates a hearing aid. Lunchtime comes and he walks towards the canteen but instead of stopping for a sandwich he walks right out onto the street. He gets onto the tube and takes it all the way to Heathrow. He gets on a plane and flies off to the other side of the world.

If he was going to do that then he would have to take a few clothes with him. So now imagine that he spent the previous evening packing a suitcase without his wife knowing anything about it, sneaking clothes out of his wardrobe while she was downstairs. Maybe he puts the suitcase in the back of his car the night before. The airlines are not allowed to tell you who checks into their flights. It's treated as confidential. If he had flown away then his passport would be gone also. But if it is still in the house it means that he never went to the airport at all.

No, he got in the car. He just walked straight out of his office and into the car park and he drove from the hospital to an unknown house where he picked up a woman and drove off. Or he stayed at hers and is there now, locked in a passionate affair. Or what if when he got into his car at the hospital there was his lover already sitting in the passenger seat, her suitcase also in the car, and they drive off together. He thinks he's in love with her and they think they are going to go forever.

Or there is no woman in the car at all and he is driving off to the middle of nowhere never to return.

No, that doesn't seem very likely at all.

No.

Chapter I

Melissa was clearly surprised to see me, her body still draped in a silk dressing gown. I entered the hallway, clumping my wet feet on the doormat.

'What's wrong?' Melissa asked.

'I need to use your bathroom.' She didn't look very happy about that.

'Is that why you were ringing the bell for the past five minutes?'

'Yes.'

'You can't go upstairs.'

'Why not?'

'Because I'm running a bath.'

'I'll only be a minute. Please, I'm dying.'

'Just wait!'

She hurried up the stairs. I could hear her walking around up there.

There was a pleasant scent emanating from the kitchen that filled the hallway. Peering into the room I saw that there was something in the oven.

'Okay, hurry up, it's upstairs on the left,' she said, running down the stairs.

'Ah, thank you.'

I headed upstairs and shut the bathroom door behind

me. The room was still full of steam, the bath full of water and mountains of bubbles. Beside the sink was what I was looking for: a plastic cup containing two toothbrushes. If David had planned ahead he'd surely have taken his toothbrush with him?

I crept along the corridor and entered the bedroom. The curtains were closed, the bed unmade and mugs cluttered the bedside table. I swung open a wardrobe and was presented with suits and shirts and smart shoes down below. It's as though David hadn't taken anything with him at all.

'Is everything okay?' Melissa called up from below.

I hurried back to the bathroom, washed my hands, flushed the toilet and hurried down. 'What a great place you have here,' I said.

She was standing at the bottom of the stairs, arms folded.

'Have you *found* anything?' she asked impatiently as I stepped back into the hallway.

'I went by David's office, met a Dr. Charlotte Bell.'

'Oh yeah? What the hell's she been saying?'

'She said she saw David on the morning he disappeared but nothing seemed out of the ordinary.'

'I wouldn't believe anything she says.'

'Why?'

'She's a troublemaker. Used to be good friends with David until she made a fool of herself, declared her love for him. It was just so embarrassing. She can't find a man of her own so she goes after mine. I mean, *really*. In the end she caused so much trouble that he just couldn't stand being around her. He couldn't wait to transfer.'

'Do you think she knows more than she's letting on?'

'I think she knows *less* than she's letting on.'

'She says that David drove to work. What kind of car did he drive?'

'A Mercedes, silver.'

'And it's been reported missing?'

'You can't report a car as missing if the owner drives it away. The owner can do whatever they want with it. '

'Is his passport still here?'

'Of course it is.'

'Can you double check for me?'

'It's upstairs in the study, where it always is.' Her face flushed. 'That's where it *always* is.' She hurried upstairs only to reappear a moment later, pale as can be. She sat on the stairs and pressed her face into her hands. 'It's gone.' She looked up at me and asked desperately, as though I had the answer, 'Does that mean he's gone too?'

'You don't know that,' I said, even though I thought she should probably trust her own instinct. 'Where do you think he could have gone? Does he have any relatives abroad?'

'His brother and mother. I mean, his brother is in Canada but I've spoken to him and he's as worried as I am.'

'And his mother?'

'She lives in London.'

'What does she know?'

'We're not exactly on speaking terms.'

'She does know he's missing though, doesn't she?' She looked at me blankly.

'Like I said we're not on speaking terms.'

I grabbed the phone in the hallway.

'I really think we should call her.'

'Now?'

'Surely she has a right to know her son is missing.'

She quickly retrieved an address book, found the number and dialled.

'Iris, it's Melissa. *Me-liss-a*. We're looking for David. Have you heard from him? If he calls you have to let me know as soon as possible, okay? We haven't seen him for several weeks now... No, no, don't get upset. I'm sure he's okay, we have a specialist looking for him and he is going to find him for us. Okay, yes, you let me know. Speak later and take care.' She put the phone down. 'She hasn't heard from him either.'

In the kitchen a timer went off.

'What's in the oven?'

'Oh, the casserole.' It had slipped her mind.

When Melissa disappeared into the kitchen I quickly picked up the phone and hit the redial button. The voice that greeted me was far more automated than I had expected. 'The time is... two... forty... six... p... m.' The address book still lay open. I put the receiver down, flipped open my notebook and quickly copied down the number.

Chapter J

Miles upon miles of cars spread out from the little booth into the far distance.

'I'm looking for a car,' I said to the guy behind the murky glass.

'You lost your car?' he asked.

'This is the registration,' I said, sliding the piece of paper beneath the glass.

'When did you drop it off?' He typed the number into his system.

'End of October.'

'October?' He pointed to a sign behind him. Every word was in block capitals. 'It says right here, maximum stay of three weeks,' he said, raising his voice. 'You're supposed to go on holiday and come back, not disappear forever.' He hit a key. 'It's not in our system. Look, after three weeks we make contact with the owner but if it's still here after four weeks the car's impounded. If it's not picked up after another month, they crush it up into a little cube. What kind of car was it?'

'Mercedes.' He looked sick.

'How rich do you have to be to forget your Mercedes?'

'Could you let me in and let me take a look back there myself?'

'No way. No one's allowed back here.'

'I could make it interesting for you.'

'How interesting?'

'All ten pounds interesting.'

'Make it fifty and I'll let you in.'

'Fifty? I've only got twenty…' I fished around in my pocket and pulled out some coins, '…four, thirty-five.' He rolled his eyes.

'Hand it over.' I pushed £24.35 under the glass. 'Why the hell did you leave it here in the first place?' he asked as the gate lifted.

'Forgetful, I guess.'

'You've got thirty minutes before my boss gets back from lunch. Hurry up.'

Planes roared overhead, obliterating all other sound around me. I wandered along rows of every kind of car imaginable. Silver Mercedes popped up everywhere, waiting for me around every corner, each one a mismatch of the registration number. I must have walked for several miles and soon enough the guy from the booth came running over to me, totally out of breath by the time he reached me.

'I thought I said thirty minutes?' he said, his hand pressed against his chest.

'I've just got a few more rows to get through. Then I'll be out of your way.'

'You'll get out of here right now. My boss is pissed and I've had to leave the booth unattended to find you.'

'Just two more rows and then I'll…' He grabbed my coat. I couldn't make out the expletives. At that very moment a plane surged overheard and blasted them all out.

Chapter K

I entered the phone booth and dialled the number from my notebook. The first words I heard were:

'David?'

'I'm afraid not. My name is Eugene. It's David I wanted to ask you about.'

'Who did you say you were?'

'My name is Eugene Blake. I'm looking for David.'

'Are you a friend of his?'

'That's right.'

'Where do you know him from?'

'From school.'

'He never mentioned a Eugene. I have a good memory, you know.'

'Well we weren't *close* friends but we sat together in history.'

'I can take a message for you if you like and pass it onto him.'

'You're in contact with him?'

'That boy never calls. I just sit here waiting for the phone to ring. Half the time I think it's broken.'

'He hasn't been in touch at all?'

'That's David for you.'

'Do you know what's happened to David?'

'Happened? Is something wrong?'

'I'm afraid to say that David is missing.'

'Missing? David?' I was surprised to hear her kick up a laugh. 'He's not missing. He's on a business trip.'

'A business trip?'

'Yes, of course he is. In Germany.'

'When did he tell you that?'

'The last time he called, a few weeks ago.' I was scribbling frantically in my notebook.

'Did he say where he was going exactly?'

'One of those grey cities. Stuttgart, Cologne, I can't remember. I was just trying to remember this morning as a matter of fact.'

'Listen, would you be free to meet up for a cup of coffee? I'd like to ask you a few questions.'

We met at the Piccadilly Cafe on Denman Street, that little cafe that opened in 1954 but hadn't changed a bit. You could still get egg and chips for £3.50. I found Martha White tucked into one of the booths there and she'd already discoloured to match the greying wall behind her.

'Are you the man on the telephone?' she asked.

'Yes, I am. Nice to meet you.'

'What was your name again?'

'Eugene.'

'Eugene... Oh yes, of course. I usually have an excellent memory. I don't know what's wrong with me these days.'

I slid in opposite her.

'Thank you for seeing me at such short notice.' I took out my notebook. 'Do you mind if I ask you a few questions?'

'I do if it's on an empty stomach!' She clicked her fingers, summoning a waitress and it wasn't long before there was a large battered cod swimming in chips and tartar sauce sitting in front of me. She had the same. All around me diners were tucking into similarly gigantic portions.

'I like good appetites. My David was always so *fussy*. I like a boy who *eats*.'

'Oh, I can eat,' I said. I almost didn't have to ask any questions as she just launched into answers to questions I hadn't actually posed, as though all these words had been building up inside her for years and she just needed someone's attention to let them out.

'When I first came to this country I did not know what to make of it. The streets were not paved with gold like my father told me they would be before we left and I had never known such dreary weather! For a little girl who loved the sun I could never forgive my father for bringing me somewhere so grey. I'd never seen so many clouds before, didn't know what fog was. So I was in this miserable place and I had been cut off from all my friends, from everything I had back home.

'But when I eventually had David everything burst to life. I was just so happy, me and him against the world. But time races by and babies grow up far too quickly and children have no idea what their mothers have done for them. And he transformed from a delightful boy into the most difficult teenager you could imagine. He never listened to me nor to any of his teachers. He was always on the verge of being kicked out of school but the secret was that beneath it all he hid a fierce intelligence. All his teachers were gobsmacked when he emerged from the examinations with three As and announced to everyone he was going to study medicine. No one believed it or could understand why. He had never shown an interest in becoming a doctor before but he worked intensely for ten years and achieved his goal, just as he said he would. It was almost as though he did it just to defy the naysayers. I always say he must be the most selfish doctor the profession has ever seen.'

'Why do you say that?'

'Because he's forgotten about me. Every morning I wake up and I think maybe this is the day he'll call but he never does.'

'What did he say about this business trip?'

'Just that he was going to Germany but I told him to call me as soon as he could when he got there.'

'And did he?'

'Not a word.'

'Did he go on many trips like this?'

'From time to time.'

'And how did he seem when he told you this?'

'The strange thing about it was that he told me in person, showed up at my door, which was odd. I don't remember the last time he did that. We had tea and biscuits, watched a bit of TV and then almost as soon as he had arrived he was gone. I treasure the hug he gave me. That was rare for him, he was never a very affectionate boy.'

'So you think he's disappeared to Germany?'

'He can't still be there after all this time.'

'Well if he's not there, where could he be?'

'Have you spoken to Melissa?'

'It was Melissa who asked me to look for him.'

'Look, when he was a boy he would disappear all the time. Whenever things got tough, whenever there was

something he didn't want to deal with, he'd run away.
He'll show up. Mark my words. That boy will show
up.'

Chapter L

The rain was blackening the city as I tramped through it, my collar pulled up and my shoes soaked through. I ducked into The Bricklayer's Arms to get out of the rain and thought about what I had learned over a pint of their cheapest lager and a packet of pork scratchings. I took a first gulp of the pint and rested it delicately on a beermat and then knotted my brow in preparation for the thinking through of the puzzle.

By the time I made it through my pint I had had no ideas except to order another. By the end of my second the only idea I'd had was to order a third and two further packets of pork scratchings. But when leaning on the bar and sticking my hand into my raincoat pocket I did not pull out my wallet but instead a crumpled piece of paper and a book of matches, recalling only then that I'd found them in David White's jacket.

I sat down with the third pint and made good progress on it as I toyed with the book of matches. Flipping it open I noticed that each match was still in tact. The front was graced with the illustration of a dragon while the back announced the name of the restaurant: The Jade Palace. I returned it to my pocket and uncrumpled the piece of paper only to find that it was a receipt. I dropped it back on the table in favour of porky snacks.

It was only as my fourth pint was coming to it's natural end that my eyes fell on the receipt again. It was a receipt for a book purchased at Quinto Books on Charing Cross Road. 'Phillips, J. Van…' was all it said due to the limited character space. But as that fourth pint started to go to my head I did spot something else: the date. It was a date in September, not long before David's disappearance. Charing Cross Road was not very far so I decided to finish up my pint and march through the rain along Tottenham Court Road to a bookshop that is now long gone.

It was close to nine by the time I got there and they were getting ready to close.

'Excuse me,' I said. 'Have you got anything by J. Phillips?'

'J. Phillips? Never heard of him,' said the gruff man with a heavily-lined face and close-cropped hair.

'You sold one here in September.' I showed him the receipt.

'No idea,' he said.

'Please, can you check? It's a matter of life and death.' I think that was the fourth pint talking.

'Well I've got a problem, you see. We've gone and got a new computer. Got to get with the times and all that but the student who is entering all the information is the only person who knows how to use it and he doesn't work today.'

'Well, could you try?'

'Why's it so important? Is it a gift or something?'

'Something like that.'

'If it helps you get her into bed then I'll help you otherwise I don't see the point,' he grumbled as he limped over to the computer. 'Now, let me see here,' he said, putting on his huge, square glasses. 'He told me what it was I had to press.'

'I use computers at work. I could give it a go.'

'No, no, no, keep back! No one is allowed back here.' He typed a few keys. 'Phillips D, Phillips E, Phillips F. Here it is... Phillips, James; Phillips, John; Phillips, Joseph. Which one are you looking for?'

'I don't know.'

'Well you're no help.'

'Can you give me some titles?'

'*Cooking for One; The Art of the Sandwich; Microwave Mastery; Vanishing Acts; Advanced Skiing Techniques volume 1; Advanced Skiing Techniques volume 2.*'

'Wait a second, what did you say?'

'*Advanced Skiing—*'

'No, before that?'

'*Vanishing Acts.*'

'That's it. That's the one. Do you have a copy?' He hit a couple of keys.

'According to this... downstairs, room 3, non-fiction. Phillips, John.'

'Thank you,' I said, running down the narrow stairs past the 'No Bags' sign and into the musty rooms below, each one stuffed from floor to ceiling with tatty paperbacks. The scent of decaying pages was thick in the air as my eyes scanned the shelves of the third room along. I trailed the authors until I found Phillips. And there it was. I stretched on tip toes to pull it down. *Vanishing Acts: a guide to disappearing completely* by

John Phillips. I flipped it around in hope of finding a photo of the author.

Chapter M

It was a doorway on Berwick Street with a series of buzzers for film labs and editing suites. In amongst them were three letters scrawled in biro on the buzzer label: 'Alter Ego'.

I buzzed and a voice crackled through.

'Hello?'

'I have a nine-thirty appointment.'

'First floor. End of the corridor.'

I walked up the creaky, carpeted staircase and along the landing to a door with no sign at all. I knocked and a voice from within told me to enter.

A brunette in a cat-print blouse sat at a desk. The minuscule room was almost entirely bare except for a telephone and a couple of chairs. She was leafing through a magazine.

'I'm here for the nine-thirty appointment.'

'I know,' she said with a smile, revealing her braces.

'My name is…'

'That's ok.'

'You don't need my name?'

'Nope.' She just continued to smile.

'If you take a seat then he will be with you soon. He's just got someone with him at the moment.'

I sat on one of the little plastic chairs and looked around the room.

'Cold today, isn't it?' she said.

'Very.'

'I hate the cold. I always tell people I was born in the wrong country.' She laughed just to dissolve the silence.

'I don't mind the cold,' I said.

'Oh,' she said, and stopped laughing.

'What does VPA stand for?' I asked the receptionist.

'I don't know.'

'You don't know?'

'I've never asked.'

'How long have you been with this company?'

'Over a year.'

The door to the next room opened and a tearful woman dressed in black came out, a clump of tissues in her gloved hand.

'Next!' I heard a voice say.

'He's ready for you now,' said the receptionist.

I entered and closed the door. John Phillips was standing by the window looking out. I sat on the chair in front of his large desk.

I had a moment to observe him because he wasn't saying anything at all. He was maybe around sixty, with greyed stubble and a tendency to breath heavily between words as though speaking was a real effort.

'It's that parking attendant. The same one every day. She doesn't know anyone can see her circling, waiting for the meters to run out. I've even seen her write a ticket, wait for the very second it runs out, and slap it onto the car. And that was my car. At two I'll be running down to put more coins in the meter. I've got my eye on her. You want to disappear.' He now seemed to be talking to me but hadn't turned from the window.

'Yes. I want to disappear,' I said.

He sat down at his desk across from me and took off his glasses. His eyes seemed to be distracted by something in the distance before settling on me. 'You don't want to disappear.'

'No?'

'Get out of here. Sort your problems out the real way. Take your head out of the sand and face them head on. What is it, money? Family? No, with you I think it's woman trouble. You look like the sort.' I couldn't tell if he was being sarcastic. 'You're in love with her but she's dangerous and you want to get away, to disappear forever.' He was way off but I thought it might be wise to humour him.

'How did you know?' I asked.

'I can tell.'

'You can tell all that just by looking at me? You must be a very good judge of character.'

'Character is my business,' he said. 'And I'm telling you now, disappearing ain't cheap.'

'I'll pay. Whatever it takes.'

'I'm not talking about money. I'm talking about character, resilience. Do you have what it takes? In this business you pay with your life, with your identity. Everything you've worked on up to now will be wiped out. You will no longer be the man sitting in front of me but someone else entirely. You love your mother, right?'

'Excuse me?'

'If you love her, get out of here. Go have a drink, see a movie, do *something*, because the one thing that is guaranteed is you'll break her heart. You'll be leaving her behind in her own world and she'll have no idea what happened to you. She won't know if you're dead or alive and until the day she dies it will fill her every moment with sadness. It's the main source of regret for many of my clients and I don't want you sitting in that chair in a year's time asking me to undo it all.'

'I've never known a company to talk you out of paying for their services.'

'I learnt pretty quickly that people aren't built for this kind of thing. You're born empty, grow a personality and it's then almost impossible to rip that personality away from your body; it's a tricky suture to unpick. You have one name your whole life and then to be given another poses a serious psychological challenge. You no longer have your childhood friends, your brothers, your sisters. All ties are severed. If you have kids, you'll never see them again. It can break people emotionally and I found I had to start by talking people out of it because they just couldn't take it. They'd come back to me six weeks later telling me they wanted their old life back. But it was too late by then. Every trace of them was already gone.'

'How do you do that? How do you get rid of every trace?'

'There are different ways. Some are easy. Change their look, change their clothes, colour their hair. People are creatures of habit. They have their favourite coat, their favourite pair of shoes. We bin them. In fact we get rid of all their clothes. By not allowing them to wear a single stitch that they owned before, they get the sense of being an entirely new person. If they usually dress smartly, we make them dress casually. If they're usually a mess, we sharpen them up. But this is all superficial. We can then take it to the next level and change their name legally. And they don't even get to select it. I choose it. I found that if you let someone choose their own name, they come to me with some ridiculous movie star name. No, it has to be a name that fits, something relatively anonymous. Another James Smith walking around's not going to cause any problems. We can then go even further, get rid of all their bank accounts, their medical records, have them disappear completely.'

'What do you tell the family? Don't the banks ask questions?'

'There are levels of disappearance. It depends if you want any answers to the question of their disappearance to be left behind. You can have someone disappear and provide zero answers as to where they went. They will remain a mystery for the rest of time.'

'What about the police? Don't they suspect anything?'

'Do you know how many people go missing every year? If someone doesn't want to be found then there is nothing they can do. Especially if it's a bloke. It's the women and the children they're concerned about.'

'So they just become a mystery and no one ever knows what happened to them?'

'Well there are yet more extreme ways, where we provide an answer to that question.'

'How?'

'You can make it appear as though they met their maker. Either by accident or by their own hand. But I really wouldn't recommend it. It's a messy business and *expensive*. So tell me... do you still want to disappear?'

'I'm looking for a man called David White,' I said, removing the photo from my coat and laying it on the table.

He went silent. 'Do you know him? Did he come here?'

'I don't talk about my clients.'

'You have to tell me. I have to find him.'

'You're not the first, you know.'

'Not the first to look for David White? Who else is looking for him?'

'What you're doing is absolutely futile. You will never be able to find him. If he came in here at all, that is,' he said, getting up. 'Now, if you'd excuse me, that shark is circling again and I have coins to slot in the meter.' He pulled open his drawer to reveal that it was full of twenty pence pieces.

As I walked out the receptionist was ripping out a page from the desk diary. Walking along the hall, I heard a shredder whir to life.

Chapter N

The table was crowded with vegetable spring rolls, pork dumplings, seaweed, egg fried rice and chicken chow mein. I piled the food onto my plate, circled it with soy sauce and snapped apart the wooden chopsticks. It was only when I was chomping away that I noticed how this Chinese restaurant looked like a former greasy spoon cafe with its formica tables, plastic benches and panel lighting. Inside only a few tables were occupied and outside the rain attacked the laundrette across the street.

The waiter passed my table, a huge guy well past six foot and well past caring. My mouth still full of food, I stopped him.

'You know this guy?'

His eyes drifted to the photo in my hand. He just shook his head, turned and disappeared into the kitchen. At that very moment a man sat at my table. He was smartly dressed in a navy suit and burgundy tie. But his hair was a greasy mess and the bags under his eyes made it look like he hadn't slept for weeks.

'Just my luck,' he said to himself. His eyes locked onto mine. 'Just my luck,' he repeated.

'It's just one of those days when all your luck has run out. You know those days when every last drop has dripped away? My wife is going to bury me because I have finally done what she told me not to. I have lost every last penny to our name.' He pushed his greasy hair away from his forehead. 'She told me not to touch the savings and she was right. Rachel's always right. But I thought all I needed was a drop of luck.'

'How did you lose it?' I asked as I stuck another dumpling in my mouth.

'You wouldn't think it to look at me but I have a disease. You know, I *wish* I was an alcoholic. At least then I would have drunk myself to death a long time ago. What I have is much worse. I am addicted to a dream… the dream of money, mountains of it. Can you imagine that a simple pack of fifty-two cards can lead to such devastation? The very same pack of cards that magicians use to perform tricks at children's parties?'

'You lost it here? In this place?' He looked around before leaning in and lowering his voice. His eyes narrowed.

'You may have noticed that the kung pow chicken tastes a bit like cardboard, that the seaweed is a bit powdery, that the miso soup tastes canned. Well that's because it is. This may look like any other Chinese restaurant to you. It might even taste and smell like one to you but what you have really walked into is an illusion.' The chicken tasted fine to me. 'They don't trade in chicken; they trade in men's souls and tonight I've traded mine.' I didn't bother to ask him what the hell he was talking about. 'They are watching you, you know. The very fact I am talking to you brings you under suspicion. I wouldn't order any more if I were you. I would eat up, put some money down for the bill and calmly walk out of here.'

'I need to show you something,' I said. I held out the photograph.

'Put that away!' His eyes scanned the room. I stuck it back in my pocket.

'You know him?'

'You can't just go flashing photographs like that in here. It's not good for you. It's not good for *me*.'

'You've seen him before?'

'Not for a long time. I don't know the guy's name or where he's from or where he went, I just know I've played him.'

'*Played* him?'

'Upstairs. I lost the lot but he won big. Not that he was particularly good, just a lucky so-and-so. That guy must have been a saint in a past life to be handed so much luck in this one. But sometimes that luck can work against you, especially here. You want just enough for the right hand here or there. With too many hands you look like a big shot and they start to think you are destined for better things.'

'Better things?' I had started in on the chow mein. He was right: it did taste a little bit like cardboard.

'They ship you off.'

'Who does?'

'*She* does.'

'Who's she? David was shipped off?'

'Is that his name?'

'Where to?'

'Some fancy places. He's probably out there now, living the high life, with everything he could possibly want. Champagne, all the girls he could handle. Well, either that or he's faced-down in a gutter, his soul slipping away in a stream of blood. It just depends how

70

long his luck holds out for.'

'Can you tell me where he is?'

'He's in another league now. You'll never find him. He's in some of the most exclusive rooms in the city and there's no way you'd ever get in. Not dressed like that anyway. Where *did* you get that coat?'

Neither I nor the stranger noticed the hand before it was already gripping his shoulder.

'I hope this degenerate isn't bothering you.' That huge waiter had returned.

'No bother,' I said. 'Lilly would like a word with you,' he said quietly to the stranger.

'Don't you think ruining me is enough? What more does she want from me?'

The waiter pulled him right up off his chair. 'Just hurry up. Hey!' he yelled to a waitress. 'More dumplings,' he said, nodding his head towards my table.

A little panicked, I ate the dumplings as quickly as I could and stood up to leave but now it was my shoulder that the meaty hand gripped.

'This way,' said the barman.

'Excellent dumplings by the way.'

'This. Way,' he repeated and pushed me all the way to the back of the restaurant. I headed through the kitchen where cans of miso soup were indeed piled up everywhere, and was pushed up a cramped staircase. As I walked along a corridor, a glance in one of the doorways revealed a number of men - and men only - around a green felt table, quietly concerned with the hushed flipping of cards and clacking of chips.

At the end of the corridor was a partially open door. The barman went ahead of me and knocked.

'Come in,' said a woman's voice.

His look was enough to instruct me to do what the voice said so I entered and the door locked quickly behind me. The little office room was scented with jasmine and behind a desk sat a young woman, her sharply-cut, jet-black hair framing her smooth skin and perfectly-placed features.

'Sit down, please. I apologise for having to bring you up here like this. I don't like to bother the customers when I have business to take care of. Would you like anything? Tea?'

'Oh no, I just ate.' I sat in a deep leather armchair.

'I personally find these games so silly and more trouble than they're worth. I'd much rather get straight to the point. Leon was saying you have some information that could be of some use to me.'

'Leon?'

'Your friend.'

'I've never seen that guy before.'

'I am looking for this Mr. White and I believe you can tell me where to find him.'

'I think there has been a misunderstanding. I have no idea where he is.'

'But isn't that a photograph of him in your pocket?' I didn't answer her. 'I find it strange that you would walk around with a picture of a stranger in your pocket if you don't know where he is. Are you his brother? Are you also a Mr White?'

'I don't know what that guy was telling you, but...'

'He told me *everything*,' she said, interrupting me.

'I don't know who that guy was.'

'I don't believe you.'

'Look, I don't know what that guy has been telling

you but I really don't know where he is. In fact I am looking for him myself.'

'He owes you one hundred thousand pounds too?' That shut me up. 'We had an agreement. He broke the terms of our agreement. I helped him out, you see, sent him into the upper echelons of society. But for every hand he wins I am to receive a share. Of course, it's my money he's gambling with and gamble he has done. He's been putting everything on single hands, trying to bluff his way to victory. But I don't like liars, Mr. White. Lying will get you nowhere. He lost everything. And once the money disappeared, so did Mr. White. So now I would very much like to have my money back so you will now tell me where your brother is.'

'He is not my brother.'

She called to the waiter outside, who entered quietly, shut the door behind him and waited patiently.

'Tell me where he is and it will be so much easier.'

'I don't know where he is!'

All she had to do was glance at the waiter and his concrete fist was across my jaw. I saw stars.

'You tell me where Mr. White is,' she said again.

When I could speak again I tried to get out as many words as I could. 'I am looking for him too! I have never met him before but I've been asked by his wife to look…'

The fist interrupted me this time with a crack to my skull. This dislodged an idea and sent it spouting out of my mouth. I didn't quite know what I was talking about.

'Tell me where you sent him. Let me into his world and I will bring him back to you.' The room disintegrated around me.

He grabbed the lapel of my raincoat but she stopped him.

'Wait. Your idea interests me. I have thrown one man to the lions, why not another? You go tonight, I give you money to play with, and you bring White to me.'

'Wait wait, wait - "money to play with"?'

'Of course you will play. You *know* how to play?'

'Of course I do.' I had no idea.

'You will go now. Zhang, take the car.'

I was manhandled into a car in front of the restaurant. When it moved it sliced right through the city.

'Where are you taking me?' I asked, nursing my jaw.

'You are very foolish to get involved. You don't see what's happening?'

'No, what?'

'You're being fed to the lions.' That phrase again. 'You cannot compete with these people. If you think a little slap hurts, wait until you get punched by a bullet.' He had done far more than slap me. The city looked awfully blurry through these eyes.

'Be a good guy, let me out and we'll forget the whole thing. I can even give you the loot.'

'I'll pretend I didn't hear that.'

'Just tell them you were letting me out of the car, we had a tussle and I ran off.' He laughed.

'If we fought there would be no escape for you.'

'You've got the money with you?'

'She's arranged everything. It'll be waiting for you when you get there.'

'Get where?'

'You'll find out soon enough.'

The car shot through the city and strangers and

storefronts and buildings floated past and the greyness fell away; stone was replaced by glass and the modern world towered around us. Skyscrapers brushed fog and random squares were lit amongst the grids of offices where workers pulling all-nighters deteriorated at their desks.

We glided deep into this futuristic world and pulled into the entrance of a hotel.

A uniformed valet opened the door for me.

'Good evening, sir,' he said. It was my moment to run but that fist grabbed my arm and escorted me into the bustling lobby where guests were going about their evenings, unaware of the fate of that fat man in their midst. Zhang exchanged a nod of familiarity with a lobby boy. They must have all been in on it.

At the lift he produced a key card from his wallet.

'This will take you to where you need to go, all the way up.'

'You aren't joining me?'

'I'll be parked right outside and watching, so don't even think about escaping.'

The panel in the lift listed numbers one through fifteen and I watched each light up but when it got to fifteen it didn't stop until it travelled somewhere far beyond.

The doors opened to spread a luxury hotel suite out in front of me. A fully-stocked bar ran right along one wall, leading to the panoramic window that presented the lights of London. A large fireplace dominated the opposite wall and sofas and armchairs were arranged at its centre. I wandered from room to room, each one as empty as the last. I found a small screening room with twelve tiered seats and a cinema screen that took over one wall. The marble bathroom revealed two sinks, a huge walk-in shower and a stand-alone bathtub. And in the bedroom I found a giant, fluffy bed. I flipped off my shoes, climbed under the covers and drifted away.

Chapter O

I emerged from sleep to find a man in a white shirt, black waistcoat and bow tie, physically shaking me.

'Your table is ready, sir,' he said. 'Sir,' he repeated, 'your *table*.'

For a moment I thought I had fallen asleep in a restaurant and was forcibly being shown to dinner.

'I don't remember ordering anything,' I said as I tried to soak up the room around me.

'We will be starting in a moment,' he said, and disappeared.

I sat up and realised I had slept in my clothes, raincoat included. I fumbled around with my shoes and glanced in the mirror only to find my face discoloured by sleep and bruises.

I emerged from the bedroom to find that the waiter wasn't a waiter at all and it wasn't a dinner table he was showing me to. Right in the centre of the room, where the sofa had been, was a large poker table.

'What do you expect me to do with this?' I asked him.

'Play!' said a voice. I turned around to find another man standing at the bar fixing himself a drink. He was wearing a pristine white suit over a white shirt and white tie.

'What's going on?' I asked.

'Oh, that's good,' he said, as he removed the concoction he had mixed from his lips. 'I'm making you one of these. Ever had a Devil's Kiss? I just invented it.' He stirred a couple of cocktails. 'Oh, and I'm sorry we're late, I had to stop off at the dry cleaner's.' He looked at me properly for the first time and with that he lost a little of his energy.

'Where are they finding these people?' he asked the croupier. 'What the dickens happened to your face?' He stepped out from behind the bar.

'A little altercation.'

'What's the other guy look like? You should really put some ice on that.' He looked me up and down. 'But more importantly where *did* you get that coat?'

'Ealing,' I said.

'You look like that guy, what's his name...' He pinched between his eyes. 'Used to be on telly.' He handed me one of the cocktails. 'Try that.'

A sip was enough to ignite my throat and set me coughing.

He whacked my back as he laughed.

'What... the hell... is in that?'

'Oh, that *kick*? Just a couple of drops of ghost chilli extract. Half a million Scovilles. That's why it's named The Devil's Kiss. I kind of like it,' he said, sipping his delicately.

I had stopped coughing but he felt the need to whack me on the back once more before heading over to the table and taking his seat. I dragged myself to the table and sat opposite.

'Is it only us?' I asked.

'You were expecting someone else?'

The croupier was winding off the cellophane from a fresh pack of cards. He was a man so spindly that he looked like he had smuggled his clothes from his father's wardrobe.

'Your credit has been arranged, sir,' he told me.

'How much will I be playing with?'

'Fifty thousand,' he said. Those words gripped me. It was more money than I had ever had in the world, several times over.

The croupier shuffled with finesse, his hands moving at such a high speed that the cards blurred and with the speed of a gunslinger, he tossed them out our way.

It turns out that relaying poker games hand-by-hand is incredibly boring. Trust me, I tried to give you an action-packed rendering of what occurred that night in the hotel suite but it just wasn't possible. You should see all the crumpled up balls of paper around the room.

I did have an immediate problem. I didn't know how to play. Not in real life, anyway. As I lifted the edges of the two cards in front of me my brain was frantically rushing through the corridors of my mind in search of any clues as to how to play, yanking open filing cabinets that spilled forth all sorts of irrelevant information. I remembered the cake at my fourth birthday party, the sensation of falling into a lake in Dorset at twelve, and the pin number of a long-expired debit card. And then I found it: all those unearthly hours at university glued to a primitive computer game called *Poker v1.1*. That's what I meant by 'not in real life'. The problem was that when I played I kind of guessed my way through. You could click away frantically and win hands and if I lost everything I just clicked 'New

Game' and carried on clicking. You would have thought that after hundreds of playing hours I would have picked up the actual rules? That part was sketchy.

I remembered pairs being important - two of the same's a good thing, right? And face cards - kings, queens, jacks - they're good too, yeah? Help me out here. And then there are those hands in the movies, the ones where the villain has an unbeatable hand but then the hero somehow has an even better one. I couldn't exactly remember which ones those were.

When we started playing I made losing look easy. Small pots, yes, a hundred here or there, but I was losing fast. And that's when he started talking to me. About really irrelevant things: about cheese; about safaris; about Paul Newman movies.

'He really shows you how to be a man in those movies. *Cool Hand Luke*, *Butch Cassidy*, *The Hustler*. Ever seen *The Mackintosh Man*? He's a spy and even though he's one of the good guys he ends up in prison and there's nothing he can do about it. Gets out though. I'm not spoiling it, that's half way. I'd say if you had a favourite Newman movie it would be *Harper*.'

'Never heard of it.'

'Oh man! You should catch it next time it's on TV. He plays this guy investigating a case. He meets Lauren Bacall who throws him into a web of intrigue through the streets of Los Angeles. I really think it's something you'd be into.'

He slammed down his cards and raked in the chips.

'I'm looking for someone,' I said resolutely.

'Aren't we all?'

'I'm pretty sure you know him.'

'Oh really?'

'You probably met around a table like this but he might not be using his real name. Outside of here he's just a normal guy.'

'Whatever makes you say that? If you make it in here there's nothing normal about you.'

'David White.' Saying his name didn't illicit any response at all.

'I have a rule when playing. I don't ask personal questions. I would urge you to do the same.'

'I'll tell you anything you want to know.'

'You shouldn't. When you move in these circles the last thing you want is for anyone to find out anything *real* about you.'

'What does that mean?'

'This David White, he owes you money, right?'

'He doesn't owe me anything. I just want to know where he is. He's missing and I'm looking for him.'

'Is this a joke?'

'No.'

'I mean, are *you* a joke? Look at you in that coat, talking as though you are some sort of detective. I know more than you think.'

'Oh yeah?'

'David White sat right where you're sitting now. Only difference is he actually knew how to play. Dressed more sharply than you ever have and unlike the others, instead of keeping quiet and squirming in his seat when he had a good hand, he wouldn't shut up. But people liked him. He was funny, a real crowd-pleaser. Except when he won, of course, and he would win *big*. I've never seen such big hands won by someone who sweated so little. He'd just waltz through the game, sweep up everyone's chips and disappear. Even when we were raided he didn't break a sweat.'

'Raided?'

'With all this money floating around it's a real hot-spot. Masked men with guns burst in on one game, took everything we had. They even pulled the Rolex from my wrist and fractured my nose. Joke was on them though. Watch was fake. Sadly the nose was real. But this place... try and infiltrate here and you could get your face torn off.'

'*Really*?'

'Half the guests in the lobby are security. Try and get past them, I dare you.' He started to laugh, to cackle. He had a terrible laugh. 'I'm going to give you a word of advice.' His laughter died down until there was not even a smile left in its wake. 'You really shouldn't trust people so much, shouldn't believe everything you hear. Especially around a poker table. Every word uttered is designed to deceive and distract.'

'Now I don't know if I should listen to you or ignore you.'

He picked up a stack of chips and threw them into the centre of the table. 'Raise,' he said.

Conversation faded. The croupier flipped out cards as fast as he could. Quick, short hands passed, little pots lost one after the other. But then the stack of chips started to increase, from hundreds to thousands.

The poker chip is a deceptively simple device. Without actual cash in front of you, it just becomes play money. There is no connection between those chips in front of you and those notes in your wallet. But just two of those plastic discs, worth a fraction of a penny, represented a month's salary to me.

And as I continued to lose hand after hand,

something remarkable started to happen. The scales tipped in my favour. I won a hand here, a hand there, but then I started to win every hand. It's not something I could really explain but the cards just kept coming my way. I'd start off with matching pairs, meaning that luck was already on my side, and they would repeatedly be joined by a card that made up a matching trio. And I started to feel drunk on the sensation of winning. The thrill got into my hair, my eyes, my mouth. It really just twisted through me. And across the table the stranger in the white suit was not laughing any more. He was staring at me with fiery eyes as I repeatedly raked his chips towards me, hand after hand.

'This isn't happening,' he muttered.

And then a hand came to end all hands. We had both pushed almost all of our chips into the centre of the table. In my hands a jack, a queen and a king stared up at me, all dressed up in the same suit, and they seemed to be smiling. There wasn't any way I could be beaten.

He pushed all his chips into the pile.

'What you got?' he asked.

'You first.'

He laughed, spread his cards out on the table and reached out for the chips. But when I threw my hand down it stopped him cold. This time it was me who started to laugh as I raked the chips towards me.

He slammed the table, sending the chips clattering across the room and leapt up from his chair.

'This is not happening!' he screamed at the croupier. 'He isn't even who he says he is!'

The croupier looked at me, concerned. 'Who is he?'

'He's David White.'

'David White?' The croupier looked at me. I could

83

feel the sweat starting up on my forehead. The man in the white suit grabbed the table and flung it onto its side, throwing cards and drinks and chips across the room.

It left me, the fat man in the old raincoat, still seated without a table in front of me, my winning cards still fanned out in my hand.

And he flew right towards me, grabbing me by the neck and knocking me off my chair. Me on the floor, his hands tight around my throat, his face burning with rage. He gripped me so tightly that I instantly couldn't breath. In that split second I knew that he was deadly serious, that he intended to kill me. My eyes immediately bulged from their sockets and my vision hazed. I really thought that this was it, that this was my final moment on Earth. I quickly started believing in an afterlife. But the fists suddenly let go and air sucked its way back into my lungs. And the body of that stranger slumped down onto me. I coughed convulsively and through the blur of it all I saw the croupier, with his spindly frame, gripping a dented fire extinguisher.

We were both sure that the stranger in the white suit was dead but when his body started to squirm the croupier told me he would take care of it. He pushed a briefcase into my hand and hurried me into the lift where the doors cut me off from the chaos ensuing inside. I dropped down through the building and emerged out into the lobby where all eyes were on me as I hurried towards the exit. I caught my reflection in the revolving doors and saw that my face and shirt were spattered in blood. As I was thrown out into the cold London air I realised that the stress of the situation must have kicked off one of my nosebleeds. And I span around to see where the waiter's car was but there was no car to be seen. I just stumbled along the pavement and faded into the city.

Chapter P

When I got home with that briefcase in my hand I double-locked the door behind me. The hallway light surprised me by turning on all by itself.

My grandmother was standing in her dressing gown, all silver grey hair and sparkling grey eyes. Did I forget to mention I lived with my grandmother? Well, I lived with my grandmother.

'Eugene Henry Blake. Where have you been?'

'I don't have time for this now,' I said, hurrying to my room.

'You have to call and tell me when you're coming home,' she said, following me along the hallway.

'I'm in my thirties. I shouldn't have to tell you anything.'

'Do you know what time it is?'

'You're up too!'

'Why do you think I'm up? I couldn't sleep! You could have been lying in a gutter somewhere.' And then she saw my face. 'What *happened* to you?'

'Nothing! Leave me alone!' I said, shutting the door to my room and turning the key. I threw the briefcase onto the bed, unclicked the locks and opened its jaws. Her Majesty was staring up at me many times over.

There was a knock at the door. 'Eugene!'

'Granny, go away!'

'Let me look at your face. It needs to be taken care of.'

'No, Granny, please. I just need some rest. I'll see you in the morning.'

She fell silent before I heard her footsteps patter along the hall.

Now I was faced with the task of hiding all this money. I slid it under the bed and lay on top of it, hoping for sleep to take me away. But my wired brain defied my exhausted body. The whole evening had rushed through me like a freight train and I almost didn't understand how I had ended up on top of a briefcase full of someone else's money. And as I lay there the case rattled and jumped, as if doing everything it could to tell me I was an idiot for hiding it somewhere so obvious.

'What the hell are you doing?' asked my grandma as I lay on the floor of the bathroom, unscrewing the side of the bath.

'I've got to hide this,' I said.

'What is it?'

'I'll tell you later,' I said, unscrewing the final screw. The side fell right off just as the doorbell buzzed.

'At this hour?' asked my grandmother. My hand smacked the light switch and I peered down the corridor at the front door, the screwdriver still stuck firmly in my fist. Faintly through the frosted glass I could see a figure.

'Go to your room, lock the door and stay there,' I told my grandmother.

'I'm doing no such thing. You can't hide me in my

room all the time.'

'You've got to do it. You could be in danger.'

'Danger? Oh Eugene, what kind of trouble have you got yourself into?'

'Just get in there now.' She scuttled along the corridor and disappeared into her room.

The bell rang for a second time, more insistent than the first. I stuffed the briefcase into the side of the bath and just balanced the panel against it. Screwdriver in hand, I crept along the corridor, throwing my own long shadow against the wall.

'Who is it?' I asked loudly through the door.

'You have to let me in,' said a woman's voice.

I unchained the door and swung it open to find Charlotte Bell, the doctor from Eugene's hospital, bedraggled by rain and tears, standing on my doorstep.

'Can I come in?'

'Get in here, quickly,' I said. She stepped over the threshold and grabbed onto me, burying her face into my shoulder and sobbing uncontrollably. She managed to get a few words out between the sobs. 'I just miss him... so much.'

'How did you know where to find me?'

'I looked up your medical records,' she said, wiping her eyes.

'Are you allowed to do that?'

'You really need to change your diet, by the way.'

'I didn't realise this was a home visit,' I said, shutting the door.

'Have you got anything to drink?'

'I can make you a tea.'

'I meant something stronger.'

'Who is it?' called my grandmother, her head poking

out of her room.

'Just a friend,' I said.

'What friend? Does he know what time it is?'

'It's not a he!'

'What's that?' she yelled.

'It's a girl!'

'Tell her it's far too late to be calling,' she said.

'Just get back into your room.' She mumbled something and retreated.

'Oh, I'm causing you such trouble,' said Charlotte.

'That's just my grandmother, I wouldn't worry about her.'

'Is she staying with you?'

'It's more like I'm staying with her. Let me see if I can find a drink. Just head in here,' I said, pointing to my room.

'Your bedroom?'

'Yes, just wait there.'

I hurried around the kitchen, pulling open almost every cupboard to find that bottle of whisky my sister had bought me for my birthday over two years ago. I hadn't had the heart to tell her I couldn't stand the stuff.

Charlotte was sitting on my bed, her eyes wandering along my videotapes when I entered with two glasses in one hand and the bottle of whisky in the other.

I splashed the whisky into each glass and when she got the drink into her hand she knocked it right back.

'I'm so sorry for showing up so late,' she said after catching her breath. 'I just didn't know who else to turn to. I just need David back. I need you to find him.'

'I thought you and David were just colleagues?'

She straightened herself out a little. 'Look, I wasn't entirely honest with you. When you came to visit me you asked me if there was another woman. I mean, it's not something I've talked to anyone about. It's hard admitting it to myself even but I had...' she corrected herself, '*have* feelings for him. And I'm not talking about a little office crush. If we had met earlier things would have been different. I mean, he's married, which doesn't make things easy. But I've tried to get on with my life and see other people but when I'm sitting across from these guys I'm looking through them and seeing David.'

'Did he know this?'

'I wrote him a letter, tried to rationalise how I felt. But it turned out to be a big mistake, one of the most humiliating events of my life. He came into my office and told me that the feelings were just not reciprocated. But we have a connection, I know we do, and it's something he just couldn't admit because of Melissa. It seems that the both of us cannot exist at the same time. I just wish he could be honest with me, admit that there's something there. And that's why when Carly came into the picture it just destroyed me.'

'Who's Carly?'

'Carly was a hygienist who I had hired, if you can believe it. Certainly the worst decision of my life. It started as just rumours, whispers in the rec room about what she was *doing* with him during work hours. It wasn't something I thought David was capable of. That was until that day in August when I walked into his office and saw it for myself. I mean, the door was unlocked and he had patients waiting. I was just returning a file; I didn't expect to be traumatised.

'But the thing that made it so hard was that his wife was his excuse for us. He told me that the reason why we couldn't be together was because of Melissa. And then this little nothing walks in, barely twenty-five, and he's completely taken in by her. I mean I'm a professional with three degrees. What the hell does she have?

'And then I did something that David was not happy about, something he will never forgive me for. I went to Melissa and told her everything. It probably wasn't my place but I just couldn't help myself. And the next day he was possessed. He stormed into work, pulled me into my office and screamed at me. I'd never seen him like that before. I didn't know he had such a temper. He told me he was getting out of there as soon as he could, that I had betrayed him and that he wasn't ever going to talk to me again. But it wasn't my fault I was the one who he ran to whenever he had a problem. I didn't say anything when he spent all those hours bending my ear.'

'What problems did he talk to you about?'

'Can I have another?' she asked. 'I poured her a generous glass of whisky which she magically made disappear. 'David had a serious gambling problem. I didn't know how bad it was until he came to me and confessed everything. He confessed to me, not to Melissa and not to Carly. I told him everything was going to be all right, that I was going to help him. And I read every book on the subject that I could find.'

'What kind of trouble was he in?'

'He didn't have a penny to his name, confessed that he was thousands of pounds in the red. And the whole time he kept it a complete secret from his wife. Her jewellery was even going missing just so he could gamble it away. I became his confidante and that was yet another reason why I thought we had such a connection, because he trusted me with such a private secret. I made an appointment for him to see a counsellor but he refused to go, saying he had it under control, that he could break the cycle himself.'

There was a knock at the door and I saw my grandmother's face peering in.

'Go to bed, Granny!'

'Eugene…' she forced me to come closer. 'Have you offered your guest anything to eat?'

'It's almost three in the morning!'

'Are you hungry?' my grandmother asked Charlotte.

'No, I'm fine, thank you.'

I had to almost physically push my grandmother out of the room.

'Look at me,' said Charlotte, 'talking like this and it's you who needs attention. She stood up and looked more closely at my face. What happened to you? Did you get into a fight or something?'

'Yeah. It was kind of one-sided.'

'Sounds like you're having quite the adventure being a private detective. Do you have a first aid kit?'

'It's in the bathroom cupboard. I'll get it.'

'No, you sit here. Where's the bathroom?'

'Down the hall on your left,' and only as she left the room did I remember the money. I froze, waiting for her to discover it, for a gasp to ring throughout the flat but instead she just returned with the kit in her hand.

'Sit on the bed,' she said.

I did what she asked as she applied cream and then plasters to my face. 'I expect that this is just another day at the office for a private detective.'

'Yep.'

'How did you even become a private detective?'

'Let's just say I fell into it.'

She pressed the plaster to my forehead and smoothed it over. Her hands ran down my face and kissed it wherever she pleased.

Chapter Q

The next morning I walked into the tiny kitchen to find my grandmother piling up bacon on Charlotte's plate.

'What's going on here?' I asked, interrupting their conversation.

'Eugene!' exclaimed my grandmother. 'Why didn't you tell me you had such a *lovely* girlfriend?'

'Girlfriend?'

'Eugene, you never mentioned me to your grandmother?'

'He's so secretive,' said my grandmother as she cracked two more eggs into the frying pan. 'All these years we have *longed* for Geney to find a nice girl and when he finally does he doesn't say a word. Youngsters today...'

'How is that supposed to make me feel, Geney?' asked Charlotte. Only my grandmother called me that. 'And you never told me you had such a lovely grandmother.'

'See, there he goes, being secretive again. You should have seen him in the bathroom last night. He wouldn't tell me *what* he was up to.'

'What were you getting up to in the bathroom last

night?'

'Granny, I really think that's enough.'

'Your grandmother was just telling me lots of stories about you. Apparently you used to be quite the troublemaker.'

'He couldn't walk until he was two. Sit down Eugene, I've got eggs going for you.'

'I'm not hungry.'

'Well I never! *You...* not hungry? Are you feeling okay?'

'It's okay Iris... he can share mine. Bacon's not really my thing,' said Charlotte.

'You're not one of these health nuts are you?'

'I'm a doctor.'

'A doctor! My goodness. I wish my Eugene was clever enough to be a doctor but his teachers said that we shouldn't hold out much hope for him. Well my husband had a fry-up every morning of his life and it didn't do him any harm.'

'He *died*, Grandma!'

'I know he *died* but it was the smoking that got him in the end. The bacon had nothing to do with it. So eat up.'

'Don't you have to be in work?' I asked Charlotte.

'My first appointment's not until ten but you can give me a lift, can't you darling?'

'I really think we need to leave.'

'I was hoping I could have a shower.'

'There's plenty of hot water. Eugene, go get her a towel...'

'I don't think you have time for that, do you?'

'Don't mind him. He's just grumpy in the morning.' She placed a plate of bacon and eggs down on the table. 'Eat up, Eugene.'

I sped along the high street in my grandmother's car.

'What were you doing back there?' I asked.

'I was just having a little fun,' said Charlotte. 'She's sweet, really.'

'How am I going to unexplain everything you told her?'

'Like what?'

'Like I've got a girlfriend who is also a qualified doctor.'

'It's not such a terrible idea, is it?'

'But it's just not true!'

'After everything that happened last night?'

'Nothing *happened* last night.'

'I did sleep over.'

'That's exactly it. You *slept* over. Do you have any idea how uncomfortable that sofa is?'

'You didn't have to sleep in the next room.'

'I really don't know what you've got into your head but there's nothing between us.'

'There's no need to get all antsy about it. I was only playing with you.'

'Well, don't. I'm having enough trouble knowing what's real and what's not these days without you making it worse.'

'Your grandmother's right.'

'About what?'

'You really are grumpy in the morning.'

I pulled into the staff parking lot.

'I need you to do something for me,' I said. 'I need you to get me Carly's number.' Her smile disappeared.

'What for?'

'I need to talk to her.'

'About what?'

'I need to find out what she knows about David.'

Only when she left did I look up at the wall ahead of me. A plaque read: 'Dr. D. White.'

When she returned she passed a piece of paper to me through the window and placed a full kiss on my lips.

Chapter R

I stuffed myself into a phone box, my eyes crawling around the call girls plastered there. I slotted a few coins into the machine, punched the numbers and held the receiver to my ear.

'Hello?' answered a woman's voice.

'Carly?'

'No. Who is this?'

'My name is Blake. Is Carly there?'

'What do you want to speak to her about?'

'I just have some questions for her.'

'Even if she was here I wouldn't let you speak to her.'

'Why not?'

'I have no idea who you are. One of those saps from her little black book, I suppose.'

'Do many guys call her?'

'None of your business. She's not here.'

'Where is she?'

'She moved. You'd better stop or you'll be in trouble.' The dialling tone ran on.

Later, when I was back at home, my phone rang. Before I had time to say a single word: 'Stop calling here.'

'Who is this?'

'Who are you, more like? What I had with David is over. I didn't know he was married. When I found out it ended right there. He broke my heart and I never want to hear from him again. Just like I don't want to hear from you again.'

'Carly, wait, I just have to ask you someth-' *Click.* The dialling tone hummed.

I quickly dialled 1-4-7-1. 'This phone number has been restricted,' said the synthetic automated voice. I put the phone down, perplexed. Especially since I hadn't given out my number.

Chapter S

Melissa emerged from her house wearing dark glasses and carrying a large bag.

I soon discovered the difficulties of following someone. I don't know if you've ever tried it but it's surprisingly hard not to actually catch up with the person you're following. Melissa was walking really slowly and I kept having to reduce my pace otherwise I would be right up beside her. It briefly occurred to me that perhaps the activity I was engaged in was not an act of following but a crime of stalking but I assured myself to the best of my ability that I was a professional.

I stayed as far behind as I could, winding around corners and crossing the street where required. I followed her all the way along Acton High Street, across Ealing Common and across the green towards Ealing Broadway. I just could not figure out what she was up to and I started to feel that my suspicions were correct, that the clues to the case would be found by focusing on where it all started, with Melissa.

I ended up following her around the supermarket. She bought spaghetti, salad and a bottle of wine.

* * *

The next day I followed Melissa around a department store as she browsed clothes. I felt distinctly out of place when she entered the underwear department. I retreated to the mens' slippers in the corner and watched her from there. She took so long that I did get a chance to buy a new pair of socks. The ones I was wearing had holes in them.

At lunch she took me to a cafe which turned out to be excellent. She had a soup and a salad whereas I went for a chicken sandwich with extra mayonnaise. We sat across the room from each other. Afterwards we saw a movie together. *Everyone Says I Love You*. She sat towards the back but I much prefer the front so I sat in the third row. I really quite liked the movie but I'm not too sure if she cared for it or not.

On the way home she stopped at the dry cleaners and picked up some clothes and it was only as she reached home that I noticed she'd picked up a man's suit.

Later that evening Melissa emerged from her house still wearing dark glasses even though it was dark outside. She carried the suit with her. At the end of the road she hailed a cab and I hailed one to follow hers.

The cabs raced through the city, one on the tail of the other.

The Fairway Hotel was one of several on a seedy stretch by King's Cross where the 'No' of the neon 'Vacancies' sign was always dark. Outside they still advertised the fact that their rooms had colour TVs and their signs still contained the defunct '081' area code. I watched from across the street as Melissa entered the lobby and made her way up the stairs.

Once she disappeared I walked in myself.

'Give me a room,' I said to the concierge, who looked up from his paper.

'All guests pay first,' he said, sounding mildly annoyed that I had disturbed him.

'How much is it?'

'Thirty-five pounds a night,' he said, pointing to a sign.

His arm reached up to the keys hanging on hooks behind him.

'Room 302,' I said.

'Why?'

'It's my lucky number.' The key for room 301 was the only one missing.

He unhooked the key and hung it on his finger in front of me.

'No soliciting, no firearms and no funny business.'

Chapter T

The corridor was crowded with shadows, dimly lit by one solitary bulb at its farthest end. I pressed my ear up to room 301 and heard voices that were so muffled that I couldn't decipher the words.

My room was a sparse affair: a bed, a chair, a table and a kettle. I picked up the glass I found beside the sink, moved the chair against the wall and took my place. From there I could see the hotel across the street, silhouettes of bodies in the windows.

Through the glass I heard voices. A man was talking but however hard I strained to make sense out of the words, I could not glue their syllables together. I started to visualise an empty room, identical to mine, with only a television playing inside.

I flipped off my shoes and lay on the bed in my raincoat. I hadn't intended to fall asleep but I felt myself drifting away, being dragged under by fatigue, and the lights of the city went out one by one.

I was awoken by a knocking. I sprung out of sleep and onto my feet in one seamless motion. The knocking was coming from the wall and it transformed itself into a kind of banging, a steady *bang… bang… bang…* And then a voice started to rise, a woman's voice. Not words as such, just elongated sounds. I grabbed the glass and put my ear up to the wall once again and the moans transformed into words, a kind of *yes... yes... yes...* And then the banging stopped and a man's voice blended with the woman's. Then silence fell.

By that time it was about three in the morning. I just sat in the chair waiting for something else to happen but all that happened was silence.

I couldn't sleep anymore so at six o'clock I wandered across the street and sat in the window of a cafe that overlooked the hotel. The only other people in there were hard-hatted construction workers kicking off their shifts with thick rashers of bacon between doorstop slices of white bread. I had what they were having and the sounds I had heard lingered in my mind as I watched the light shift ever so slightly from black to dark blue.

It was closer to eight when I saw Melissa walking right out of the hotel with a man on her arm, a tall man with dark hair and dark glasses. I quickly ran out of the cafe and followed them. They were across the street and walking too fast for me. When I turned the corner they had somehow disappeared. I was left on the corner, a fat man doubled over and out of breath.

I headed back to the hotel and saw there was a new face at the reception, a young kid who couldn't have been many days over eighteen. I hurried in, breathless.

'I've forgotten my wallet and my wife's waiting for me, I've just got to pop up and get it.'

'Sure, what number?'

'301.'

He handed me the key.

I hurried along the corridor and stealthily unlocked the door to room 301.

I scanned the room. The curtains were open and the morning light flooded onto the bed where the battered sheets, duvet and pillows mingled together. There was no suitcase, barely any sign that anyone had been there. Yesterday's newspaper was on the side-table. I picked it up and noticed that the crossword had been half-finished. I opened the cupboard, empty except for a single suit. I took the jacket off the hook and checked the pockets. Nothing. It was a nice dark grey jacket. I tried it on and the lining ripped as I tried to slip it over my shoulder. I returned it to the hanger and shut the wardrobe.

In the bathroom all I found was a toothbrush and a comb.

I'm not sure what I thought I would find.

There was a knock at the door. I froze and allowed silence to saturate the room around me. Another knock, louder this time.

When I heard a key slipping into the lock I ran into the bathroom, turned on the shower and frantically started to undress myself. The next knock I heard was on the door of the bathroom and it reverberated against the tiles.

'Sir!' It sounded like the kid from reception.

I kept silent.

'Sir!' he repeated. I jumped in the shower. It was freezing but I managed to at least get my hair wet. I shut off the water.

'What is it!' I yelled, sounding as pissed off as I could.

'I think you've made a mistake!' yelled the boy from

the other side of the door.

'I'm in the shower!'

'I know but I think you're in the wrong room.'

'What the hell are you talking about?'

I got out, wrapped a bright blue towel around my waist and swung the door wide open. He quickly averted his eyes.

'What is it?' I said, sounding appropriately annoyed.

'Uh...' The boy didn't know what had hit him. He'd never seen so much flesh in one place before. 'I'm sorry to disturb you, but this is not your room.'

'Not my room!' I marched over to the front door clutching the towel tightly at my side.

I pointed to the door. 'Look, its... Oh...' I laughed a little. 'I'll get dressed and come down to reception. I have to check out anyway.'

'What about your wife?'

'Well she is a very patient woman.'

When I got out of the hotel I was still buzzing with the thrill of it all. I jumped on a bus and just let it take me wherever it was headed.

The view from the top deck allowed me to contemplate what I had seen. Who was this man who had been with Melissa? If David was having an affair, did this mean that Melissa was having one too? I felt I was onto something.

Chapter U

When I got back to my grandma's flat the front door was already open ahead of me. I stepped inside.

'Hello?' I called.

The door of the living room was wide open and books had been pulled off shelves, the side table was upturned and my grandmother's ornament cabinet was empty, all her sentimental little trinkets scattered around the floor.

I ran into my grandmother's room to find her sitting quietly in her armchair, intensely studying a copy of the *Radio Times*.

'We've been burgled.'

'When?'

'Last night, this morning, I don't know. Didn't you hear anything?'

'I thought your room was looking no more untidy than usual this morning.'

I ran along the corridor to my room. The mattress was off the bed and my wardrobe had been completely emptied.

'You really thought I left it like this?'

'You have to admit that you are very messy,' said my grandmother.

'Not this messy!' I ran into the bathroom to find the bathtub completely intact. I knew from that moment that I had to do whatever I could to make sure my grandma was safe.

'Carol?' I said down the phone. 'It's me, Eugene... It's about grandma... No, she's fine, I just need you to take care of her for a couple of days. We've been burgled and I don't think she's safe here. It won't be long, I just need to change the locks and get everything in order... I'm bringing her around right now. Yes, it has to be tonight. We'll be there in thirty minutes.'

Chapter V

When I returned home I could hear the phone ringing on the other side of the door. I rushed inside and snapped it up.

'Eugene...' Her voice was weak.

'Yes?'

'They've found it. They've found the car.'

'Where?'

'I need you to take me...' Her voice went faint. These words were all she could manage.

'Don't move. I'll be right over.'

I was out of the door almost as soon as I had put the phone down. My grandmother let me borrow her car whenever I needed it, a trembling white hatchback bought sometime in the late eighties. That boxy old thing was as shaky as I was as I drove recklessly along the quiet residential streets.

Melissa's eyes were all used up from crying.

'We have to go down there now. We have to see it.'

'Maybe it's best if you stay here and wait for news.'

'I'm not going to sit here and *wait* for things to happen. I have to know. I have to see it for myself.'

'Where is it?'

She seemed to grow faint and dropped on the sofa,

her head squeezed in her hands. I hurried over to her and was about to touch the flesh of her arm. 'It's in the water,' she said.

'The water?'

'They're trying to pull it out as we speak.'

'Is there any...? Is he...?'

'I wanted to thank you,' she said, looking up at me with those emerald eyes.

'For what?'

'For everything you've done. You came to my aid when I needed you. Nobody else did.'

She shook herself out of it. 'Look at me, being so silly.' She swiped away her tears and rose to her feet. 'We're wasting time. I have to see it. I have to see it with my own eyes.'

Only the silvery rectangle of roof was visible. It was only natural that all the other parts that make up a car should follow below the murky surface. Rescue workers in blazing orange overalls buzzed around us, some submerged up to their waists while others, fully decked out in wet suits, only had their heads above the water. We came to the clearing to find them in the middle of attaching a tow cable to the car somewhere underwater, the other end of which was attached to a monstrous tow truck that had sunk itself securely into the sludge. The air was raw, the wind edged with ice and the trees that surrounded the lake bent towards us to get a good look at the scene that had disturbed their peace.

We were not very far outside of the M25, that tarmac streak that circles the city, and the lake really wasn't very large at all. The visibility of the car's roof proved just how shallow it was at its centre. From the main road we were a good ten minutes' drive and we had to wind through a maze of lanes to find it. But if you listened quietly you could still hear the faint roar of the motorway in the distance.

I stared at the car and contemplated how it could have possibly got to where it was. It was almost more reasonable to imagine it falling out of the sky than for it to have been driven all the way to the centre.

Melissa was frozen, her glassy eyes wide as they glared out at the water in front of her. The freshness of her face was replaced by a muted greyness as her composure slowly decayed. I put my arm around her and her body softened, melted a little into me and her shivers transmitted right through to my body, shivers of fear rather than of cold. Her mouth was open as if she was about to utter something but no sounds escaped. It felt as if she wasn't really there at all.

When I said 'it's going to be okay,' I didn't really know what I meant. Most likely I was just reassuring myself because nothing was okay. Nothing was at it should be. A car was in a lake, a girl was in my arms. All the laws of reality that I had taken for granted had been broken.

A police officer took her away and talked to her quietly and after a while it became apparent that it was proving difficult to get that wreck out of the water.

I wandered up to one of the workers who was beside the rescue truck.

'Do we know if there's anyone in there?'

'There never is when we pull these things out. Can't tell yet anyway. Water's so brown it's impossible to see anything at all down there.'

'Do you know how long it's been in there?'

'Could have been weeks. Was only spotted this morning by a lady walking a dachshund.'

There was some commotion in the middle of the lake as the divers moved out of the way and the truck on the bank whirred to life. The winch started to crank and a creaking emerged from the water as the vehicle was forcibly tugged out of the earth below. I watched the winch slowly turning on that truck as it pulled those cables in and as the car moved closer towards the muddy bank the water lowered from around it. Second by second a little more of the vehicle was revealed. The back window was too dirty to see through. What had once been pristine silver car was now a murky black.

I hadn't noticed a ghostly Melissa stepping towards to the bank. The car was closer and all the back windows were now above the surface. Suddenly Melissa bolted towards the car, the workers failing to grab her. She splashed into the water right up to her waist and manically swiped the passenger window with her hand. I wasn't in the right spot to see through the window myself but I could see Melissa's face. I saw it contort with horror and her piercing scream sliced through everyone there. Melissa disappeared into the black water, arms groping at her from all sides to pull her out.

As she was dragged out the winch on the truck continued to turn, inching the car closer towards me. My eyes were fixated on the window that had been made clear by Melissa and as it came closer I could make out a body and as it came closer I could make out a head and as it came closer I could make out an expression: a bloated face, skin the shade of death, a rigid mouth stuck open, eyeballs wide and glaring.

My search ended here: a drowned body in a metal coffin.

Melissa was driven off in an ambulance and I waited and watched the activity.

I overheard a couple of workers.

'It's strange.'

'What's strange?' asked the other.

'It's not that deep. We've pulled cars out of water like this before but they've always been able to get out in time. This guy, it's like he wanted to be in there.'

The words wound their way through me as I looked down at my shoes, almost completely submerged in the mud.

I drove mindlessly away from there, barely paying attention to where I was going, just powering along the motorway, my foot as far down as it could go. I just wanted to drive, to get lost, to erase this whole ugly business from my mind. I was angry at myself for having started this whole charade in the first place. This was really nothing to do with me and yet I had gotten myself entangled in it all. And I was no longer the distant observer looking into the case from the outside. The case was now inside me and it was shredding me all up. And after anger came sadness, sadness that such a thing could happen in the world, that a man could be driven to end his life in such a way. I imagined the pain that David White must have experienced to have come to such a disturbing conclusion and I thought back through my life at what I thought were moments of despair but none were so bad that I ever contemplated ending it all. I would rather be left down and out than to choose to leave this planet.

The whiney roar of the engine drowned out all sound except for the whirring of my brain. His final moments seemed so calculated, like an act that would require an unusual amount of determination. There was no sudden ending, no stepping off a platform or clicking a bullet into a gun before pulling a trigger. This was an ending of *design*. He would have had to have decided to disappear, then seek out a lake, then slam his foot down with such determination that it sent the car flying into the water. The force would have to have been so great that it would have sent the car drifting towards the centre of the lake to where the water could reach over his head. And he would then have had to battle it out, to face the horror of the water rushing through the car. And as I drove I imagined the same water spilling in, seeping through the door, the floor, the engine, its icy coldness rising from my feet to my legs, to my body, and the scent of the water, the strangeness of having water inside your car. And I imagined the water up past my stomach, past my chest, right around me, covering the passenger seat and the glove compartment and the tape deck. And then me, still powering along the motorway, the speedometer ever-increasing, with water splashing at my hands now, covering the wheel, and those horrific final stages: pushing the door to try and get out, screaming for help, the windscreen masked by water, the freezing cold up to your chin, your lips, your nose, then only your eyes above the water, and then total submergence. I held my breath five... ten... fifteen seconds, but that was all I could take. I couldn't take the horror a second more. As I flew along the motorway I let the water spill from my car, screaming out behind me and soaking the road.

I sat frozen, my hands gripping the wheel, parked at the far end of an M25 service station. By the time I had come to a stop I had convinced myself of the sheer implausibility of such a suicide. I could no longer see how it was possible to put yourself through such a horrific experience and if it was indeed not possible then that changed everything. The suicide would therefore not be suicide at all. The whole scene became a fiction to me, a fiction made believable by the lake's authenticity as a lake, the car's authenticity as a car and the corpse's authenticity as a corpse. They each played their role perfectly but it was surely merely a role they were playing. Let's not forget, after all, that I was complicit in all this by doing my very best impression of a detective. I felt I had driven myself into a parallel world where I was the only person who suspected the truth. The only problem was that I had no idea what the truth actually was.

Chapter W

Melissa mourned in style: a delicate black veil that floated over her eyes.

She stood at the podium in the ornate chapel and gathered herself before speaking.

'I'm just so glad you could all be here to honour my husband and I know that David would have loved to have been here himself. He was my soulmate, my guardian angel and the love of my life. I don't know what I am going to do without him.'

She spoke with confidence. The fragility she had displayed as she had approached the podium gave way to an unexpected ease in front of the crowd. 'It was eight years ago when I met David at a medical conference. He asked me directions to one of the lectures which just so happened to be the same one I was attending. We sat together and afterwards David bought me coffee and told me that he had had no intention of seeing that lecture. I mean, how interesting can molecular biology be? But he sat through those two and a half hours just so he could buy me that coffee.

'And to tell you the truth I didn't even like him at first. I found him kind of arrogant, so I played hard to get. *Really* hard to get. And I was impressed when he persisted because I really didn't think he would make it. We would make dates and I would cancel at the last minute; I would shut the door on him just as he was going in for a goodnight kiss. I'd pretend to be busy even when I had absolutely nothing to do. But he won me over. What I took for arrogance turned out to be confidence, a confidence that I started to find charming. It was exuberance, a passion for life, which I think is why he became a doctor. He wanted to know what made people tick. He had a genuine concern for his patients, a real compassion for people he had never met before. That is why he dedicated his life to helping them.

'It was music that led him to the study of the ear and to audiology. He was fascinated by sound and by the primal connection between humans and music. He wanted to know why it resonated so deeply with us, why these sounds seemed to cut to the core of the species. He would always tell me that if music had been uninvented then humans would very quickly re-invent it, that it was fundamental to our existence.

'And that's why music was so sacred to him. We had a piece of music that connected us. He played it to me the night he asked me to marry him and I was so moved when I heard it playing as I walked down the aisle. That's why I will be playing it for you now, to honour him.

'I cannot believe that he has left me. They call them life partners but that is a misnomer. Life partners can be taken away from you at any time so it's worth spending as much time as you can with them while they're around. I just wish I could have done something differently. I knew he was suffering and I tried to help but it just was not good enough. I wish I could go back and show him how much he was loved and how much he would be missed. To see you all here, he would have been so pleased. If only he could be here himself.'

The music started over the speakers: Mendelssohn's Violin Concerto in E Minor with its rising strings and crashing chords, and Melissa headed back to the pews where comforting arms surrounded her.

While the music played I looked around the congregation. It struck me that there weren't really many people there. Mourners were scattered across the first few rows. It was a sorry-looking bunch and not really the type of gathering you'd expect for a man who, from Melissa's description, was supposed to be so compassionate and caring.

What also struck me was that people I had expected to see in attendance were nowhere to be seen. Charlotte, for instance, the woman who claimed to have had feelings for David. Surely she would have shown up. But even more puzzling was that David's mother wasn't there.

As the music continued I tried to imagine that body I had seen, now dried out, lying there in that wooden coffin. Did it still have that frozen look of horror on its face? And instead of looking like it was trying to escape from a car did it now look like it was trying to escape from a coffin?

I watched the congregation filter slowly outside as

the wooden box was lifted and carried reverentially towards the open grave. I followed but kept myself at a distance as I watched the mourners surround that hole in the ground. The sky, which had been clear earlier, now threatened rain. The coffin was slowly lowered into the grave and Melissa was the first to throw earth over it. The others followed.

One of the men started to walk away, a grey-haired man in a brown suit. I caught up with him at the gate to the cemetery.

'Heading off?'

'I don't mean to be disrespectful but I have a class to teach and I'm already late. I'm glad I was able to come and pay my respects.'

'Do you mind if I walk with you?'

'Not at all.'

'It's such a tragedy, wouldn't you say?' I asked him.

'Oh yes. Such a shock.'

'Did you know David well?'

'I worked with him about twelve years ago. We were never particularly close but we kept in touch, talked maybe once a year. It just came as such a shock, so out of the blue, that I thought I really should come and pay my respects.'

'So you didn't see him regularly?'

'No. And this is the first time I've met his wife. Very striking woman. And so tragic for her.'

'I hope you don't mind me saying this but there was something I found quite strange about the funeral...'

'That there weren't many people there?' he said quickly, as though the same thing was on his mind. 'I was wondering that too. I had a word with another chap, a guy he'd been to university with. Again he also did not know David very well.'

'Does that not strike you as odd?'

'It certainly does.'

'How did you find out about David?'

'Melissa called me last night. I was quite taken aback. I hadn't spoken to David in maybe two years and hadn't seen him in maybe twice as long as that and here was his wife on the phone to me, not only telling me that he had died but that the funeral was the very next day. To tell you the truth it all rather shook me up. I think I am still in a state of shock.'

'And what did you think about David's mother not showing up?' He looked at me with incredulity.

'His mother?'

'Isn't it off that she didn't turn up to his funeral?'

'But David's mother is dead.'

'*Dead*?'

'Yes, didn't you know?'

'Who told you that?'

'Melissa, just now, when I asked her. She told me that David had no surviving parents, that his mother had passed last year.'

'That's not possible. I met David's mother and while she may not be in perfect health, she's most certainly alive.'

I returned to the gate of the cemetery and watched the crowd thin out until there was no one left. I took that opportunity to look more closely at the open grave.

That wooden box was lying deep beneath the ground, superficially covered with scattered earth. I wondered how long the box would survive, not to mention the body within it. How long would it be before that body is consumed by the Earth, eaten through by those minuscule creatures that live below ground?

'What are you doing here?' I turned to find Melissa.

'I came to pay my respects,' I said, almost genuinely.

'What more do you want? He's been found, hasn't he?'

'He certainly has.'

'Then there's nothing more you could need. The case is closed.'

'There is one thing,' I said.

'What's that?'

'I haven't been paid... yet.' She held her handkerchief to her face as the tears started to roll.

'I can't believe you could ask such a thing on a day like this.'

'I didn't mean to upset you.'

'No, it's okay. I suppose some people are just heartless.' She straightened herself out. 'Come to my house. Not tomorrow. Thursday. You can have your precious money then.'

Chapter X

To me he was as solid as the oak wardrobe he stood in front of. Nightly I would awake to find the shadows of my room dominated by a single shadow, darker than the rest. Like a photograph emerging in chemicals he began to crystallise out of the darkness. And there he was in my room. David White, as dead as can be.

I say dead as can be because it was certainly not the alive David White that stood before me. Yes he was standing and yes he was staring but he was a kind of copy of David White, the corpse version, the one from the car; bloated, soaked through. And when my eyes adjusted it was clear that his skin was as blue as this ink. And the more he visited the clearer it became that he was decomposing, a horrible, withering version of him that stared right into me. Those were nights of terror, of cowering sweatily under the duvet. That was until I discovered that he was as scared as I was, a realisation that calmed my shredded nerves a little. And it became clear that he was trying to tell me something. His silvery eyes glinted.

I sat up in bed, bunching the covers at my chin. 'What do you want? Why do you keep bothering me?'

He struggled to form words with his colourless lips and dead tongue. All he could manage was, 'P-p-p...'

'Spit it out,' I said. I was a touch impatient come to think of it.

'P-p-p...' he said but he couldn't get out more than that staccato sound and when he tired he started to fade. Either that or it was me who faded.

The next morning I marvelled at the soggy patch of carpet he left behind as well as the shadow burnt into the wardrobe.

Later I discovered that these visions weren't nightmares but night terrors, a phenomenon far more vivid than mere dreams. Eyes open but brain playing tricks. So between the unreal corpse following me during my sleeping hours and the live body that would come to follow me during my waking ones I could feel myself coming apart at the seams.

One night I slipped on my raincoat and headed out the front door. It didn't help that the shadow that had been burnt into my wardrobe came with me. It followed me all the way to the station where it waited patiently on the platform and when I stepped onto the tube it did the same. I watched it at the empty end of the carriage, cancelling out all the light around it.

When my stop arrived I dashed off the tube as the doors started to shut, catching my raincoat in the process. I yanked it out of there and saw the shadow stare at me helplessly as it was sucked into the tunnel.

Melissa's house was in darkness and the longer I watched the longer I could not discern signs of life. An eerie emptiness had fallen upon the whole street and even the air seemed peculiarly still. I rang the doorbell repeatedly but there was no answer. I dialled Melissa's number on my fat mobile and let it ring until there was no doubt that the house was empty, that Melissa was no longer to be found there.

Chapter Y

A sickly yellow light buzzed through the foyer of the Fairway Hotel.

'I need some information,' I said to the clerk. I held a five pound note in my hand.

'Rooms are £35 a night,' he said in a thick accent. I couldn't place it.

'It's about one of your guests.'

'I can't give out any information about our guests. Confidential.'

I flattened the fiver down on the counter.

'That guy in Room 301. He's still there?'

'Room 301?' He knew who I was talking about. He glanced down at the note and then back up to me. 'What's it to you?'

'I've got a problem you see. A *marital* problem.'

'That's none of my business.' I found a twin for that fiver.

'How'd you feel if that guy in Room 301 was seeing your wife?'

'I really wouldn't like that.'

'You've seen that redhead in here, right?'

'That redhead's your wife?'

The fivers became triplets.

'You can tell me anything.'

His hand covered the notes and he made them disappear. 'Sure, she was here. But you're out of luck. He checked out already.'

'When?'

'Yesterday.'

'And she was with him?'

'Yeah.'

'Do you know what they were arguing about?'

'I gave up eavesdropping on guests years ago. You can really get into trouble for that kind of thing.'

'Do you have any idea where they were going?'

'How should I know?'

'They didn't mention anything?'

'Nothing.'

'Did you ever see what they were up to?'

'He hardly ever left the place, kept himself to himself. I only saw her a few times. Heard them arguing though.'

'Really?'

'Yeah. Some of the other guests complained about the noise they were making.'

I rapped my fingers on the counter. 'So what are you going to do when you catch him?' he asked.

'Oh, I'm cooking up something, let me tell you.'

'You'd better really let him have it. Not *guns* or anything, just fists. How can you put up with him sleeping with your wife like that?'

'It's not really up to me.'

Later that night I could be found wandering the streets, turning corners on a hunch rather than by design.

I was all out of ideas.

I meandered past the cinemas of Leicester Square with their lighted marquees and promise of escapism inside. The movie posters boasted of the adventures you could be a part of but I was no longer interested in adventure. A quiet life was starting to sound pretty thrilling to me.

I headed off the square and discovered a library. It seemed appropriate that a man bled dry of ideas should stumble across a building full of them.

The library was dark, the atmosphere hushed in reverence. There was some kind of performance going on. Listeners sat cross-legged on the floor, aimed towards a corner where a skinny poet was illuminated. Little poems with no rhymes at all pinged out of his mouth. I listened for a moment and discovered they were about as interesting as a shopping list.

I wandered off to explore the darkened stacks, creeping along the carpeted rows flanked by ceiling-high shelves. The rows seemed to go on forever and I followed them far into the darkness until I could no longer hear those prickly little poems anymore.

I discovered I was in the crime section, faced with a collection of books that looked like they hadn't been touched in years. Each hardback had been plastered with a sticky protective film which seemed to destroy the book rather than protect it, wiping out the pleasurable texture that came from holding a book naked, as it were. Why not just let the dust cover do its thing? You wondered how people treated books once they got them into the privacy of their own home. Behind closed doors they are subjected to all kinds of horror: cracked spines, coffee rings, ink tattoos.

I pulled down a hardback from the shelf. *Bust Out*, it was called. The cover was graced with an illustration of a prisoner in black and white stripes gripping a smoking gun. The return slip was almost entirely blue with date stamps, having been removed from this library at least sixty different times. That's sixty different pairs of hands turning its pages and sixty pairs of eyes running over its words. It's a wonder these little things can hold up to such scrutiny.

I replaced it and let my eyes drift until they caught something that had a ring of familiarity. I pulled the creased little paperback down from the shelf: *The Electric Detective* by Henry Silverling, the same book I had plucked out of that box in my dorm room. A wave of nostalgia came over me. The one I held in my hands was the very same edition I had read all those years ago.

I examined it under the light of a reading lamp. The cover was a thing of beauty: an illustration of a blonde in the shadow of a detective. The returns plate revealed that this was a reissue from Parallel Press that showed up in the library in 1971. When a few dislodged pages fluttered out I carefully slotted them back in. I even spent a moment straightening the dog ears, each one the point at which its reader had reached their stop, gotten bored or fallen asleep.

I turned to the opening page.

New York, 1941

Two sets of knuckles, one beside the other, clinging to a ledge. But not just any ledge. This one was way up.

Way above the city, the eighty-first floor of the unmade Empire State Building.

Think about the Empire State Building as it towers over the sparkling city that surrounds it. Then close in, right in, to the eighty-first floor, so many miles above Fifth Avenue, and notice two sets of knuckles, one beside the other, as they struggle to cling on. Now imagine a body down below, hanging from those knuckles. This is Jack Claw, our hero for the next two hundred pages. (Eugene's note: Don't worry, I'm not going to give you the whole thing. Just an extract.) He's not doing so well, his coat flapping in the wind, his hat already tumbling to the street below where it will land perfectly onto the head of Jimmy Valentine, raconteur and hot dog vendor. (It was all coming back to me as my eyes raced across the page.)

I flipped to another section.

The Great Lombardi was one of those phoneys that held audiences spellbound. He wore a velvet cape and hammed it up as though he was plugged into mystical radio waves unavailable to mere mortals. The audience were pea-brained suckers who probably believed in anything: clairvoyants and soothsayers, ghosts and spirits, angels and miracles. They probably even believed in Jesus Christ and Santa Claus.

Jack Claw didn't believe in any of that baloney. He didn't believe in much of anything, to tell you the truth.

'Ladies and gentlemen,' announced The Great Lombardi from the stage, 'you all walk about believing that the world is the way you see it. The streets, the trees, the skyscrapers. But I am about to prove that there is another dimension, a hidden dimension, one that only those born with very special powers can see. It's a place where all those missing things go, that invisible space in between things. And I am going to prove this not with a pack of cards, not with a handkerchief, not with a white rabbit but with a real live human being.'

From the wings appeared a blonde in a sparkling outfit with legs that streamed all the way down into her golden high heels. Claw sat up. A blonde was something he could believe in.

She wheeled on a square object obscured by a silver sheet.

'Not only is Natalya incredibly beautiful, she is also immensely talented. When she was a little girl she discovered that she had a very special gift. She found that she did not need to adhere to the laws of physics because Natalya could bend those laws. She could change her shape to fit any space imaginable. Even when she grew from a little girl to the beautiful woman you see before you she was still able to perform this remarkable feat.' Natalya pulled off the silver sheet to reveal a small wooden box. 'I am going to ask her to fit into this very box, an exceptionally small space by anyone's standards.' The audience exploded with applause.

Natalya, whose constant smile sparkled in the stage lights, lifted one incredibly long leg and stepped it into the box. This was followed by one of her long arms. She then curved her other leg to make it disappear somewhere in there. And in an unbelievable final move she curved her head back and pulled her whole body inside, leaving an upside-down smiling face looking out at the gasping audience.

The Great Lombardi suddenly cut off that sparkling face from the crowd by slamming the door shut. The crowd really got agitated when he removed a lock from his pocket and sealed the box shut. He delicately replaced the silver sheet as though he were laying a table.

'Let her out of there, she won't be able breathe!' shouted one guy who jumped to his feet.

'That's right!' replied Lombardi. 'The question is not only how does she fit in there but the second question is how does she survive? Ladies and gentlemen I first found Natalya in a touring circus that had travelled all the way from Siberia to Cincinnati by rail and by sea. So astonished was I by her talents that I convinced her to run away with me, to perform for The Great Lombardi.' This guy loved saying his own name.

'Hey, stop yapping and let her out already!' shouted another guy.

'Should I let her out now?'

'Yeah! How'd you like to be locked in there?'

Lombardi patted his pockets and found the key. When he unlocked the door and swung it open gasps sucked out all the oxygen from the room.

Instead of finding a folded-up Natalya the audience found nothing at all. An empty box stared back at them. To make the point further Lombardi collapsed the box so that there wasn't even an empty space to be astonished by.

'Ladies and gentlemen, I told you about that hidden dimension, that place only the gifted can tap into. Well

Natalya is now in that dimension, lost to this world.'
The audience muttered worryingly to each other. Even
Claw had to admit he was impressed. He stood to get a
better look at the box, to check if anything was below
it, behind it or above it. But he couldn't see anything
except for a space where a girl once was.

It was a shame that he was going to have to ask
Lombardi a few questions about his previous assistant
who had not only vanished into thin air but also
appeared five days later in the Hudson River. Claw's
great fear was that Natalya was next.

When questioning Lombardi in his dressing room
Claw really felt it was his business to find out how the
trick was done.

'How'd you do it, Lombardi?'

'A great magician never reveals his tricks,' he said,
peeling off his moustache.

'Well you're going to have to reveal this one to me,'
he said as his badge flipped open: *Jack Claw. Private
Investigator*. 'Is it a trap door?'

'No trap door.'

'A false back?'

'Not even close.'

'A mirror?'

'Look, I am a paid-up member of the magician's
circle,' he said as he removed the greasepaint, 'an
organisation that is over one thousand years old. Their
headquarters are in a goddamn Hungarian castle and in
that castle is a dungeon filled with magicians who have
revealed their secrets. If I were to tell you now a
poisoned dart would fly from nowhere and I too would
be, as you Americans say, *kaputt*.'

'You can maybe fool a gullible, small-town crowd

but you can't fool me. We both know you're a phoney.'

'What makes you so sure?'

'Because people don't just disappear.'

'Do they not?' Lombardi closed his eyes and pinched his fingers together.

'Lombardi?' He wasn't listening anymore. And then Claw saw it happening. Lombardi lifted right off the chair and floated, flying higher and higher until he almost touched the ceiling. And he didn't even need a puff of smoke to disappear. He was just there one second and gone the next.

Claw waved his arms over the empty chair. 'Lombardi? You there?'

Claw was really puzzled by the whole thing and tried to find the answer in a glass of whiskey across the street.

'I've had the strangest evening,' said Claw.

'It's not the first time someone's sat at that bar and told me that,' said the barman.

'I saw a man disappear right in front of my eyes.'

'You shouldn't drink so much.'

'No, I mean it. I was talking to him when it happened. I didn't even blink. He just floated off his chair and vanished.'

'You're talking about The Great Lombardi, right?'

'Yeah.'

'If I had a dime for every time someone came in here and told me how they had seen someone disappear I would have a few dollars. I don't go in for all that phoniness. It's just smoke and mirrors.'

'That's what I thought when the evening started but now I don't know what to believe.'

'Whatever you thought you saw, you didn't see. I've

got a brother who's into this kind of thing. Performed magic for years in front of the family, read everything he could find on magic. We went together to the Lombardi show when he was visiting and I asked him the very same thing. I asked him "How did Lombardi do it? How did Lombardi make that girl disappear?" He told me that he makes you see what you want to see. You cannot make a body disappear if there was no body to begin with.'

That sentence stopped me cold. My eyes flicked back and re-read it. Then I committed one of the cardinal sins. I underlined. It now read: 'there was no body to begin with'.

The rain pounded on me as I stalked the bookshops on the Charing Cross Road with their lighted windows and their shuttered entrances. It was as though the author of this novel had laced a clue into his book so that I could find it all these years later. I was in a daze, totally wrapped up in a story that was expanding through my brain, and now that the rain was coming down hard it didn't make sense for me to haunt the streets like a missing dog. I entered a fried chicken establishment, ordered a bucket of chicken and headed to the back of the restaurant with all the other weirdos.

As I worked through a fried chicken breast an image emblazoned itself on my brain, that of the blue bloated man slumped over the wheel of his car as it was dragged out of the lake. What if that coffin lowered into the ground was empty? And if I couldn't believe that there was a body in the coffin, how could I believe that the corpse pulled out of the wreck was David White at all? If it wasn't David White then who was it? And what to make of Melissa's reaction? She saw him and she fainted. Perhaps it was David she thought she'd seen but this was someone else entirely. But why the hell was he in David's car?

I imagined this guy before he'd become a corpse. Maybe he too is a missing person and there's someone out there looking for him right now. Maybe he has a whole family of his own who are distraught because they have no idea what had happened to their husband or father, unaware that he could be lying in a wooden box under the ground.

After the chicken I just had to have a few beers to steady myself and perhaps it was the beer that did it, or perhaps it was the chicken, but I found myself standing outside a police station.

Chapter Z

My sister always told me that I could never tell a story without missing something important. Well it's finally happened. I forgot to tell you exactly what happened to me before I became a private detective.

The dread of the working day would cripple me, would seize my arms, my legs, my chest, force my heart to pound. My vision would blur and my mouth would dry and I'd have to wait for it to pass before I could take another step. And then the blood would start its drip-drip-drop onto the pavement if I was lucky and onto my shirt if I wasn't. And this attack would hit me every day at about the same time on my morning commute, and all this because I couldn't face another day at my desk. This doesn't take into account the night anxieties, the lying awake daydreaming about nightdreaming.

To anyone on the outside looking in, they would find it hard to know what I was complaining about. I worked at a company called Curtis & Co., the head European office of a hardware supply company for the construction industry (fascinating, I know). It was my job to make sure the inventories were stocked with everything from lightbulbs to Philips head screws, from chainsaws to pneumatic drills; machine that could punch holes through the surface of the Earth. I was chained to that desk on the third floor for eleven years. Did you hear that? Eleven. Years.

My office was a putrid yellow colour because of the overhead lighting that had been installed in the swinging sixties. Life hummed and drummed in there as small talk mingled with business speak, as a disparate group of people - who would never take a second look at each other outside of the office walls - were forced to work in close proximity. And I was certain they had installed extra-small desks in there just so they could stuff more employees into one building and not have to pay for another. It meant that my arms were almost constantly in contact with Sally Price on my left and Susan Rice on my right. Yes, that was their names. They didn't see me as any kind of barrier to their small talk. I was the garden fence they talked through. I knew everything about their kids' colds, their husbands' forgetfulness, their mothers' birthdays. Their desks were cluttered with blue-tacked photos of their sons and daughters, nieces and nephews, husbands and grandparents. They couldn't bare to forget that they had lives outside of this office. All I had was a Far Side I had cut out of a newspaper and stuck to my desk. I liked the way the cows were drawn.

During those eleven years I felt like I never really woke up. Maybe it was the falling asleep at two and waking up at eight that brought it on. I felt like I was underwater in old-timey scuba diving gear. I couldn't hear or see very well and my brain was all fuzzed up. Any decision I made during those eleven years was therefore questionable. I was not of sound mind.

My boss was talking to me and I hadn't noticed.

'Eugene.' I snapped out of it.

Chester Brown was his name, which made him sound like he should have been born in the Roaring Twenties. His hobby was scuba diving and in-between business-speak he would never shut up about how it was just so freeing, how there was a whole other world down there and how you haven't *lived* until you've tried it. If you had tried it you were okay in his eyes; if you hadn't he practically held you in contempt. He even did it at weekends in a swimming pool in Ruislip, just between the granny exercise and the children's pool parties.

His penchant for swimming with the fishes, combined with a gym obsession, probably turned him against me. I was the office fatty who sat at his desk and munched crisps. He'd come into work in his Lycra gear, sweating from his gym session and shake up a protein drink which he would then proceed to slurp during his morning briefing. Oh, and he was also a dick.

He could switch from calmness to ballistic fury within a matter of seconds. A stream of rage would creep up from his neck and colour his pointy face cherry red and by then you knew it was too late because the words would be coming out in a fireball of expletives and he'd have no problem screaming at you in front of your colleagues. Oh, and he was younger than me, a full four years younger. I found it hard being told what to do by someone younger than me. I had been told how 'brilliant' he was, how he had risen up through the ranks so quickly but clearly he had bullied his way to the top. The guy also had an undeserving full head of brown hair with no signs of it receding. Some people have all the luck.

'Eugene!' he yelled. I was actually in a meeting with the department.

'Where's that report? What was the PPC for February?'

'The PPC... for February?' My head dropped to my notebook. I leafed frantically. 'It's in here somewhere.' It wasn't. The fact that I was even doing a report was news to me. I quickly guesstimated a number.

'365,' I said. It was a statement so final, so pointed, that surely no one could question it.

He just stared back at me. The room had fallen silent and all heads had turned towards me.

'Good.' He turned away.

I had gotten away with it. A minor victory, qualifying Wednesday to be the best day of that week so far.

I used to be a man with confidence, a man with hair, a man who didn't huff-and-puff when he got out of his chair. But week by week, day by day, that job sucked the life out of me. I became grey, old, apathetic, a hazy version of myself, someone I never thought I could become. And I really stopped caring.

What I'd achieved in all that time I did not know. I stuck around so long that they'd promoted me to manager, which ended up meaning even more work for me. I had thirteen people under me, asking me a thousand questions a day, burying me in queries and deadlines. People depended on me and I was losing control. Worse than that, at least in the eyes of my bosses, was that there was *money* that depended on me, which just added to the pressure.

I'd got to the stage where I'd lost so much interest in what I was doing that I started to find it hard to know *what* I was doing. I'd promise numbers, reports and results and then ignore the tasks completely. When I would talk to other people about my work I would even bore myself.

It's not like I could have gotten another job. I believed I was past my prime without anything new to offer. While to the outside world I might have passed for a man like any other but inside me ran a powerful river of anxiety, panic and hopelessness. At lunch I would sneak off to the pub at the quiet end of the high street for a pint to calm down the nerves.

It was the monotony that triggered it, the endless commutes, walking over the same pavement day after day. An hour to work, an hour back. Leaving was no longer a choice. It was something I had to do. But having been there for eleven years I couldn't find any way out. I was like someone who had done time and couldn't help but returning to incarceration. What came to be known as 'The Incident' was born out of that frustration. I had to do something drastic and I was not of sound mind when I did it. Looking back on it now some might even refer to it as a nervous breakdown, as a rupture in my life and in my psyche.

I had been awake all through the night before and the pounding in my chest had not died down, even when I was facing those stairs up to my floor.

I sat at my desk and saw that the items on my to-do list had crashed into each other. I had to unpick them apart and lay them out on a fresh page of my notebook, one by one. But I soon became overwhelmed. One task interrupted another until I found myself getting nothing done. I stared at my screen, clicked around, moved one window, re-sized another; opened one folder, closed another; anything to look like I was working. I was so tired I think I might have fallen asleep with my eyes open.

By the time the morning was over I was catatonic. Sitting in my chair, I stared at my screen, motionless.

Someone punched my chair.

'Where the fuck is that report? I said on my desk first thing. Too busy stuffing your face again? Do some fucking work. I've got the management meeting in ten minutes - I need it in my hand in five.'

'I...' I said.

'Just get on with it!'

I hadn't done the report but re-heating the numbers from last week took no time at all. I clicked Print and a helpful little message popped up:

This job has been sent to the printer.

I walked over to the printer and waited. Nothing happened. No lights flashed. No whirring began.

I sat back down at my desk and clicked Print again. The same helpful message appeared:

This job has been sent to the printer.

I stood up, walked back to the printer and stared at it. It stared back at me. I pressed a button. Nothing. I pressed another button. Nothing. Last button. Noth- I smacked the side of the printer.

I sat back down at my desk and brought up the printer queue. There they were, two jobs listed as printed and complete, as though all was well and it had done what it said it would. I clicked Print again and another popped up in the queue. I clicked Print. Yet another job in the queue. And again. And again. And again.

Now the job queue was really starting to fill up.

For tech problems the standard protocol would be to call the IT extension number. Instead I decided to handle this situation by punching the keyboard, smashing it with such force that keys flew off. Heads popped up from around the office. I grabbed my computer monitor, tore it off my desk and threw on the floor. It smashed apart on impact and some colleagues actually screamed. All of them were standing and watching: Sally Price, Susan Rice, Chester Brown, the Finance department, the Sales department, the HR department, even the Cleaning department (old Elaine with her mop and bucket) and each one allowed a silence to fall.

One voice piped up.

'Eugene...' I turned to her. 'I think these are yours.' She handed me a stack of sheets. 'They came out of the printer on my side of the office.'

'Thanks,' I said, tucking them under my arm, walking over to my boss and handing them to him.

That night I placed an ad.

Private Detective For Hire. No Case Too Small.

Chapter AA

I stepped up to the police officer at the front desk.

'Yes?' she asked

The beer wasn't really helping at this point because when my words came out they slurred.

'I'd like to report a murder, please.' The police officer glared up at me.

'Excuse me?'

'A murder. Yes. I'd like to report one.'

It only took a few seconds for another officer to pull me into the back office.

Then everything just poured out of me and I told them everything.

'...posted an ad on the internet... looked for his car... gambled in a hotel... (I failed to tell them about the bag of money in my bathroom...) flowing red hair... pulled the car out of the lake... buried the wrong man...'

By the time I had finished rambling he seemed just as exhausted as I did.

'Can I ask you a question, Mr. Black?'

'Blake.'

'Have you had anything to drink tonight?'

'Yes but that's got nothing to do with it.'

'Because it sounds like the drink is talking.'

'No, no, no.'

'I'm sure you'll agree that it's all a little hard to believe.'

'I agree. I totally agree with you. Even I find it hard to believe. But it's true, every word of it.'

'Do you like old movies? Did you ever see *Shadow Over New York*?'

'No.'

'Are you sure you haven't seen it? Because you have just told me the entire plot word for word. So next time you come in here, at least try making up something that hasn't been told a hundred times before.'

It wasn't long before I was back on the street. Across the road the shifting trees projected what looked like the shadow of a figure on the pavement. A closer look revealed that it was just a trick of the light.

Chapter AB

The next morning I was awoken by the violent buzzing of my doorbell. It kicked me right out of bed and along the hall.

I saw their outlines through the frosted glass before I saw them in the flesh. Three huge uniformed policemen.

'Yes?' I asked.

'Eugene Blake?'

'Yes.'

'Is this him?' he asked the officer at the back.

The officer from the night before didn't look too thrilled to be there. He glanced at me. 'Yeah, that's the one.'

'Get dressed. You're coming with us.'

'What's this all about?' I said as innocently as I could.

'That's exactly what we want you to tell us.'

They drove me down to the station in a fog of silence. I thought my life ended here, that Melissa's disappearance was about to pinned on me and I imagined myself staring down at a tray of grey prison food for the rest of my life. I wouldn't last a day in jail with food as grey as that.

When they got me into the station PC Morris begrudgingly took down my statement while another officer observed. I tried to make it even more convincing than the night before, adding a few exaggerations for dramatic effect. Everything about PC Morris told me that he still did not believe a word of it.

'Melissa's been missing for too long now,' I said. 'You have to go find her, check her house. Something terrible might have happened to her.'

'I don't think that's such a good idea...' said Morris, clearly not wanting to be the one to have to do it.

'Morris,' said the other officer and they exchanged looks. Morris took a second to compose himself.

'If this turns out to be a total fantasy,' he said to me, 'I am not going to be a happy bunny.'

PC Morris rang the bell and after only silence responded he swiftly followed with a forceful *rat-a-tat* on the frosted glass. The silence was almost more pronounced this time, as if the whole house was dead inside and it did its best to let us know.

'Shouldn't you shout through the letterbox?'

He shut me down with a stare, turned on his heels and started marching across the gravel.

'No, wait,' I said, following. 'Can't you bust the door down? Don't you keep one of those things in your car... what are they called?'

He stopped and stuck his face in mine. 'No, we cannot *bust down their door* just because you feel like it.'

'Can I help you?' asked a voice behind us.

We both turned back towards the house where we found the door open and a grey-haired man standing on the threshold. 'I'm sorry, I was up in my study and can't hear the bell from there.'

Morris looked at me. He presented his badge. 'I'm PC Morris.'

'And I'm PI—' He quickly interrupted me.

'Do you live here?'

'Yes.'

'How long have you lived here?'

'Almost five years. Is anything the matter?'

'And what's your name?'

'Anton Lewis. What's this about?' My neck craned to look into the hall behind him.

'If I said the name "Melissa White" to you, would it mean anything?' He thought for a moment.

'Or David White,' I added. Neither name provoked flashes of recognition.

'I can't say they do.'

'Can we come in?' I asked hurriedly.

'I *really* don't think that's necessary...' said Morris as I stepped over the threshold and hurried inside.

Instantly I saw that the painting of the lake and mountains had been replaced by a vintage travel poster for Firenze, Italy.

'This poster... how long has it been here?'

'It's always been there...'

I stepped into the living room. It was still all-white. The sofa, the walls, the fireplace, but the books were replaced with histories of the Italian Renaissance, travel guides to Italy, surveys of Italian movies. And the old maps had been replaced by family photographs.

'This makes no sense.'

'What the hell are you doing?' asked Morris.

'This is all wrong.' I knew I was going to be pulled

out of there so I hurried around the room looking for even the merest trace of Melissa or David White.

'How long have these photos been here?'

'I don't understand.'

'And these books…'

'What's all this about?'

'Do you ever subscribe to National Geographic?'

'Excuse me, detective, but have I done something wrong?' he asked me.

'He's not a detective,' said Morris.

'Then what is all this about? I live here with my wife and two young daughters.'

That didn't add up. There were no signs of children in the house. No toys, no mess, no paraphernalia. Besides, he was too old to have young daughters. His story was crumbling.

'This cabinet,' I said, rattling the roll top desk. 'Open it.'

'Open it? That's private. Tell me, what's going on?'

'Make him open it,' I said to Morris.

'Just one moment,' said Morris to the man, as he took me aside. 'What the hell do you think you're doing? This man is under no suspicion at all.'

'He *is*. He is under suspicion by me. This is the room I was in. Melissa White was lying on that couch but things were different. It's all been covered up now. Except this cabinet, this cabinet was here. It contains photos of David White. If he opens it then we have proof.'

'No one is doing anything. We are calmly walking out the door and then we are parting ways and I never want to see you ever again.' I was losing ground. Pretty soon I would have no chance of finding out anything at all.

'Tell me who you are really!' I yelled at the man. He stepped back in fear.

'I told you who I am.'

'This isn't really your house. It's a front, a cover-up. Either you have changed everything or I am going mad.'

'Then you must be going mad. I have changed nothing. Me and my wife have lived here for five years. We have two small children. She is a historian of Italian history and I am retired. This is our home and we rarely have guests. Frankly I was surprised to hear the doorbell. Now I really think you should both leave now.'

'Blake... we are *leaving*.' Morris grabbed my arm and pulled me out.

At the front door I spun around.

'There are no of signs of children...' I said to the imposter.

'Blake...,' said Morris.

'Your story doesn't hold water. This is a cover up and you are in on it. Where's Melissa? What have you done with her?'

'Blake...'

'For all I know you are an accomplice.'

'An accomplice?' he asked.

'Blake...'

'To the murder of David White.'

He looked horrified.

'Blake!' yelled Morris, yanking my arm so that I spun around.

Standing in the driveway in front of a car was a

149

woman with two little girls. The mother held them close to her.

As soon as we left Morris grabbed my lapels. 'Walk away from it,' Morris barked. 'I never want to hear from you again. Go away, take a holiday, and stop this detective nonsense. Consider this "case", if that's what you call it, closed.'

Chapter AC

Having no idea where Melissa was meant that I never got paid. I didn't want to touch the money I had hidden in my grandma's bathroom and so had to reluctantly find work quickly.

They had to send off for a special uniform. Although it was basic enough - a branded polo shirt and black elasticated trousers - their sizes only went up to XL. The HR department gloated that they were making a special, one-of-a-kind uniform that was so unique they were embroidering my name on the inside collar. When it showed up there were five XXL T-shirts and five XXL trousers, one for each day of the week. The inside collar read 'Eugene Black (*sic*)'.

I stared at myself in the mirror. The problem was that the company colour was bright orange which meant that the T-shirt was bright orange. And there is nothing worse than a fat man in orange.

The elasticated bottoms were made with a shiny, synthetic material that *swished* every time I took a step - causing a *swish, swish, swish* as I walked down the road - and which would surely ignite if they ever touched a naked flame.

There was a novelty to having a new job. My colleagues complained about it but I kind of liked it. I was out of there by four which meant I could be at the movies by five, my fist buried in popcorn. In one week I made it through *Hackers*, *Virtuosity* and *The Net* and spent the next few days dreaming about what the future would be like.

The new job meant that I was no longer chained to a desk. My desk became the moulded plastic dashboard of a white Ford emblazoned with the company's logo. It was a new chapter for me and you could almost describe me as happy.

It was only a few weeks into the job when I noticed a repeating image in my rear view mirror. In many ways it was a kind of ghost, back from the dead. Previously it had been a compressed metal cube, squashed firmly into shape by a merciless compactor. But somehow it exploded back into its original shape and sought me out in its afterlife.

It became a daily occurrence that turned into an obsession. A couple of times I'd put my foot down to try and outrun it, pulling off dangerous manoeuvres just to shake it off my tail. Fear gripped me, fear that the car I had seen being pulled out of the lake had returned to its pristine state of shining silver and tracked me as a revenge for its tragic end. The car that I had been looking for had found me.

I shook it off one Wednesday when I had a particularly large load of deliveries. I had been so troubled by its appearance that I didn't really notice where I was and it was only once I got to the building that things started to feel familiar. Luckily they had hired a young new receptionist. I dumped the packages down on the desk. 'I've got a bunch of packages here,' I said.

She read off a name.

'I'll see if I can get her for you.'

'No, that's okay. Can't you just sign for it?'

'It's policy.'

'It's not policy.'

'Susan, there's a man for you at reception,' she said on the phone, 'he's got something for you.'

Susan was certainly surprised to see me. We were never close.

'Eugene, what are you doing here?'

'I just wanted to see the old place, see how everyone is doing.'

'How are you?' she asked, stroking my arm sympathetically.

'Hanging in there.'

'I'm meant to pick up a package,' she said, looking around. 'But the guy seems to have disappeared.' It took her only a split second to notice the logo on my T-shirt. Her cheeks quickly reddened. 'Oh…'

'Sign here,' I said.

Walking back to my van I passed the silver Mercedes, innocently parked for all to see. The car could not have been a ghost since when I touched it it felt like an entirely real, physical object and not a construction of my imagination. This was the very car that had tracked me down and driven itself into my dreams. And the registration plate was a match. There was no doubt that this was David White's car.

But where was the driver? Stopped for lunch? I looked around frantically but nothing was out of order. I got back into my van and repositioned the wing mirror so that I could see the Mercedes.

After an hour I couldn't wait any longer. I was severely behind schedule and the guys at the depot were asking for me over the radio. I had to drive away from that car, knowing that it would soon be back to haunt me.

Chapter AD

When I returned to the depot that afternoon Michelle hurried to me.

'Eugene, there is a man here for you.'

'For me?'

'Yes.' It must have been the driver of the silver Mercedes.

'Tell him I'm not here.'

'He's sitting in the meeting room, waiting for you. He's been here for an hour.'

'You're not meant to let just anyone in.'

'He really was insistent. I couldn't stop him. You'd better go see him.'

The meeting room was glass and it revealed a lone man sitting at the large boardroom table, both palms flat on the surface in front of him.

He did not look how I had imagined. He had grey hair, was wearing a suit a shade of navy so dark that it might as well have been black. He was sitting with his back to the door and not even its opening or closing seemed to disturb him. I let silence linger as I contemplated what to say.

'What do you want?' was all I could come out with.

At that he turned.

'Oh,' he said, smiling as he rose from his chair, revealing himself to be somewhere around six foot. He held out his hand. 'I must apologise, I'm a little deaf,' he said as he adjusted an aid in one of his ears. 'I didn't hear you.' I looked down at his hand and up to his face. His smile continued. 'Did they tell you who I am?' I shook my head. He produced a card from his pocket and held it out between two fingers for me to examine.'

'John Jones.'

'You're not David White?'

'There's that name again. It's been following me around. No I'm plain old John Jones, one of the senior insurance investigators. I've been trying to contact you but you're a hard man to get hold of. I have a few questions for you.'

I handed back the card. 'I need you to stop following me. I need you to just leave me alone.

His smile flickered to a frown.

'Follow?'

'You can't do that to someone. You don't understand the distress it's caused me. I've been having nightmares. I can't sleep, can't think, I'm in fear for my life.'

'Fear for your life? Those are serious words. I assure you I have not been following you. But it's possible,' he said, taking a seat again, 'one of our men have.'

'Men?'

'Please, take a seat and I can explain.' I refused to sit.

He took out a notebook and unscrewed the cap of his fountain pen.

'Were you in the employ of Melissa White?'

'If you've been following me you'd know that already.'

'I have no intention of hiding anything from you.'

'I suppose my home is bugged, right? Cameras in the light switches, mics in the light bulbs?'

'Oh no, we never do anything like that. We just don't have the budget.'

'What do you have the budget for?'

'We have a select team of investigators. They go out and they watch. Yes it is true we have a file on you. I have it right here, in fact. Would you like to see it?' He produced a thin file out of his briefcase and laid it on the table. 'This is all we know but I need you to verify a few things.'

'What is this all about?'

'Melissa White.'

'I haven't had anything to do with Melissa White in ages. She disappeared.'

'Disappeared? Not at all. I was just with her this morning in my office.'

'I don't want anything to do with her.'

'Well I'm afraid you've been implicated.'

'Implicated?'

'Your name has come up several times. You're integral to her story.'

'Integral how?'

'That's what we would like to find out.'

'I haven't done anything wrong.'

'I'm not saying you have.'

'Then this doesn't concern me.'

'You were in the employ of Melissa White…?' I didn't reply but he took that as a yes. 'And what did you do for her?'

'I helped her.'

'Helped? In what way?'

'I just placed an ad, that's all I did.'

'An ad, yes!' he said enthusiastically.

'She hired me.'

'As an accountant?'

'No.'

'But you worked in an accountancy firm,' he said, checking his file. 'You took on a separate job?'

'I did.'

'And you still do this secondary job?'

'Not anymore.'

'What did you *do* for her exactly?'

'I think you know what I did. You've got a whole file on me. Surely it tells you in there.'

'I want you to say it because when I read the file I could not believe my eyes. Now I want to know if I can believe my ears.'

'She hired me to find her husband.'

'But that makes no sense. You worked in an *accountancy* firm. As an *accountant*. And not a very good one by all accounts.'

'What is that supposed to mean?'

'I've spoken to your colleagues, or ex-colleagues, I should say.'

'What business did you have talking to them?'

'I've also talked to your ex-boss and your ex-boss's boss. You certainly had quite a reputation.'

'What reputation?'

'Now don't take this personally but in an office environment everyone gets talked about behind their backs.'

'What have they been saying?'

He extracted a ring-bound flip notebook from his jacket pocket and pushed back a few pages. 'If you want to get something done, don't give it to Eugene.' He flipped a page. 'There is a collective groan when we know that Eugene would be helming a project.' And another. 'In the years he was here he redefined the idea of incompetence in the workplace.'

'They don't know what they're talking about.'

'You've been described as "burnt-out", "fatigued", "forgetful", "unpunctual", "apathetic" and "a hazard to productivity".'

'If I ever need a confidence boost I'll know not to come to you.'

'It really reads like an anti-CV. "Is no team player; a terrible communicator; consistently misses deadlines." It's a wonder you're employed at all.'

'I've been incompetent for years. That's not news. They just never fired me. I think I became part of the furniture.'

'Like a broken chair no one throws away.'

'I hated it. And there was a time when the company was about to go under and I almost found my exit. But then it somehow went from strength to strength and all our jobs were saved, without any help from me, of course.'

'They thought you were having a nervous

breakdown. Some were even convinced you were an alcoholic.'

'Who said that?'

'Is it true?'

'What?'

'You have a drinking problem?'

'Of course I don't.'

'They said you'd get really drunk at the office party.'

'*Everyone* got really drunk at the office party. That's the point of office parties.'

'When was your last hangover?'

'None of your business.'

'I see.' He scribbled something down.

'How did Mrs. White find your ad?'

'On the internet.'

'The world wide web?'

'That's the one.'

'I'm afraid I don't know very much about computers. Are you good with them?'

'Not especially.'

'What did this advert say?'

'Isn't that in your file?'

'I want to hear it from you.'

'Private detective for hire. No case...'

'*Private... detective.*' He looked awfully pleased with himself. 'Those were the words I was looking for. You, a private detective *accountant*. Tell me, what qualifications do you have for such a role?'

'It was my first case.'

'But you're trained?'

'I have experience.'

'What kind of experience?' Those paperback books I'd read, but I couldn't exactly tell him that. 'Because I find it remarkable. An office worker like you posts an ad on the world wide web and sets off for a life as a private detective. What was it, the daily grind got too much for you? You needed a life of adventure? I know what that feels like. I mean, I'm in *insurance*, the most boring job in the world. I've spent many an hour staring out of my office window, let me tell you.'

'What's this got to do with me?'

'I'm just trying to get the facts straight. What did Mrs. White tell you about David White when you first met her?'

'Not very much, that he'd disappeared and that she was worried for his life.' He wrote a line down.

'Worried for his life?'

'Said he had been depressed, that it was not like him to disappear.'

'I suppose I could ask you if it is like anyone to disappear? I mean, who disappears often? You either disappear or you don't. Did she seem upset?'

'She wasn't crying if that's what you mean.'

'How was she then?'

'Nervous.'

'Nervous how?'

'On edge. Distant, even.'

'What made you accept the case?'

'I felt bad for her.'

'So you wanted to help her?'

'Yes.'

'And didn't you think it strange that she offered you

the case, that it was you she selected to look for her husband?'

'Strange?'

'That out of everyone in the world, she hadn't gone for someone with more experience?'

'She was desperate. She needed help and I was going to do my best to give it to her.'

'And you didn't feel there was anything wrong with taking money from this desperate woman?'

'I didn't take any money.'

He let out a little laugh.

'You mean you didn't even get paid?'

'I'm still waiting.'

'Let me tell you that there is very little chance of that happening.'

'Why do you say that?'

'Melissa White does not have a penny to her name.'

'I just wanted to help her.'

'You "just wanted to help her",' he repeated as his fountain pen made its way across the page. 'That first day investigating, what did you do?'

'I don't see what this has to do with you.'

'There's a lot of money at stake here and I don't like the wool being pulled over my company's eyes. With no experience, what did you do, where did you go and what did you find out?'

'I went to where he worked. The hospital. Spoke to Charlotte Bell.' He wrote down the name. 'I didn't get much out of her. She corroborated the story, showed me the CCTV footage of David leaving the surgery.'

'Did you see his office?'

'Yes.'

'How did you get in?'

'Dr. Bell let me in.'

'Remove anything?'

'Didn't touch a thing.'

'So you walked around pretending you were a private detective, just speaking to whoever you wanted to? Who else did you talk to?'

'David's mother.'

'David's mother? Are you sure?' he asked, flipping back part of the way into the file.

'Yes.'

'That's strange.'

'Why's that strange?'

'Because I also spoke to her and she didn't mention you.'

'Well maybe she didn't want to tell you anything.'

'You must have not left much of an impression. And what information did you glean from her?'

'Not very much.'

'What information *did* you find? Your whereabouts have been hard to pinpoint except Melissa White told me that you were there when the car was pulled out of the lake. And how did you know that the body had been found?'

'Melissa called me.'

'So Mrs. White told you?'

'Yes.'

'So it seems to me that your "investigation" didn't get very far at all. Our men have been reporting that you have been walking the streets aimlessly at night, not doing very much at all. It doesn't look like you are much of a private detective. It might even be fair to say that you are a charlatan. What would you say to that?'

'Look, I might not be much of a detective but that does not make me a charlatan.' He started to pack his things together.

'Is that it?'

'Yes. I have enough.'

'Enough? Do you not want to know more about the case?'

'There is no case. I have all the information I need about the case right here,' he said, tapping the file. 'I just had to find out what kind of detective you claim to be.'

'Why is that important?'

'There are holes in Mrs. White's story. She claimed that there was a witness, a private detective. She believes that hiring you would be proof that she was really trying to look for her husband.'

'But she *was* really trying.'

'There are just too many red flags. I don't know the full story and I don't intend to find out but I do know that this meeting has confirmed that we have a case for *not* paying out.'

I sat in the darkness that evening, a drink in my hand. I thought about that file on me. How long had they been following me and how much did they know about me? Did they know about the money? And then everything became a conspiracy; in my mind they were now in the room with me when I won those hands. Now the man in the white suit opposite me was no stranger but a crony of John Jones, a planted agent with every intention of sussing me out and getting as much information out of me as possible. Now it was no longer a gang who had broken in here but the insurance agency. They knew the money was here and they were looking for it. I now felt a presence, an understanding that John Jones had been in this room.

The phone rang. I answered it.

'Hello?' I asked. Silence responded. 'Hello?' I repeated.

'Hello Eugene.' A man's voice.

'Who's this?'

'I think you know who this is.' I didn't. 'It's about Melissa.'

'What about her?'

'She's in trouble and needs to see you. Tonight. She'll be at Cafe Bruno at eleven.'

'Who is this?'

Only the dialling tone responded.

I stood there with the phone receiver in my hand, strips of streetlight stretching across my room. And then it came to me. I grabbed the mouthpiece of the receiver and tried to twist it off with all my might. I whacked it against the table, tried to break it in two over my knee. I resorted to throwing it on the floor and stamping on it until it cracked open. Fishing through the innards I tried to find it but I had no idea what it looked like. It all looked like phone parts to me.

Then I stood on a chair and unscrewed the lightbulb. Nothing seemed out of the ordinary but I dug at the light fitting, jabbed at it with a screwdriver. I just couldn't tell if it had been tampered with or not. I ended up taping over the hole just in case and then proceeded to unscrew every lightbulb in the flat and taping up all the fixtures.

I pulled out my drawers, patted around inside, raked through my clothes. I stripped my bed, slashed a knife through the mattress and felt around inside. I unplugged and dismantled my stereo and then my television. I removed all the sofa cushions and pulled a knife through them. I pulled everything out of my wardrobe. I picked at a loose piece of carpet and pulled it right across the room until all the floorboards were exposed. And I jammed a screwdriver between them and started pulling them up. I shone a torch down below but couldn't see a thing.

I was surrounded by clothes and carpet, by a dismantled radio and television and a destroyed bed. I checked my watch and realised I was late. I grabbed my raincoat and headed out the door.

Chapter AE

The city finally did it. It turned to black and white. Colour drained out of shop windows, out of the eyes of strangers, out of the hulking red buses that travelled through the night. And the night's black became deeper, became an all-enveloping darkness and sucked me right into it. The lights of Piccadilly shook off their colours, let them fall towards Eros. The red circle and blue bar of the tube signs faded. The murky brown water of the Thames took on the colour of night, a blackness that could swallow you up and lose you forever.

A series of late night cafes dotted Soho, beams of light in the darkness, where shadows of men nursed coffee. Heads against walls, heads on tables, as murky sleep took over. They brought the price of coffee down overnight; a pound a cup to drag you through to dawn. Looking around at all those amongst me, I felt the fear and loneliness so acutely, deep within my chest. It might have been the night that had coloured my thoughts during those hours but I felt like I could not go home again, that I could never be my old self again.

At eleven there was no sign of Melissa. In the corner I noticed a man ordering coffee after coffee and leafing through a newspaper. From time to time he'd look up at me and I'd avoid his glance. They were the kind of glance that he didn't want me to see, that he didn't think I had seen. I looked over at the other side of the room. Two men were sitting opposite each other and not saying a word to each other. One of them looked at me, then looked away. He glanced over his companion's shoulder at that man in the corner, who looked back at him, over to me and then back to his newspaper. Another man, by the door, also looked over to me but this time it wasn't a glance. It was a stare.

Was everyone in this cafe watching me?

I slid my coffee cup away and as I did so it seemed as though everyone in there moved a little. I shot up from my seat and headed for the door. The man by the door stood up and I bumped into him on the way out.

Now out on the street I looked back to find him following me. My walk became more of a run. I turned the corner and hid myself in a doorway.

I watched him look around desperately. When he walked off a perverse idea occurred to me, that I could turn the table on him, that the pursuer could become the pursued. The fear vibrated through me but the *idea*, the idea interested me so much that I just had to put it into action.

I stepped out of the shadows and started to follow him. To me he was just a black coat in the landscape, the outline of a man in motion against the dimly lit streets of Smithfield. He rushed past the meat market where only a few hours later butchers would descend to fill its cavernous interior with all kinds of dead meat. He dashed past the all-night Smithfield Cafe where taxi drivers congregated around styrofoam cups of sugary tea and as I continued the shadow became a touch darker. Looking up, it loomed above me, the concrete fortress of the Barbican, its three triangular towers reaching into the sky. That shadow of a man slipped through a crack in the concrete and disappeared into the maze within.

I slipped in after him.

The concrete was brown by day but by night it took on the blackness of the sky, muddied only by the sickly yellow light that dimly illuminated its cloisters and walkways. A utopian vision out of the past filled the present with a kind of horror, the concrete arches and towers baffling anyone who entered it. You could be lost in there for days, a sense I felt acutely as I stalked its terraces and passageways. I passed the units of flats with names such as Defoe House or Bunyan Court, all former residents of this patch of the city. Down below a church still stood and beneath it were buried the remains of John Milton.

With its patches of nature, where by day ducks float by and residential children play, it was designed as a place you would never want to leave. With its hundreds of parking spaces underground, its little gardens and hundreds of living quarters up above, it was meant to contain all that you could ever require for modern living. A shopping centre was planned one level below ground but the plan was unrealised, leaving an unutilised concrete passageway only to be filled with offices years later. And bridges that took you 'directly' via a zig-zag of passageways to the Barbican and Moorgate stations envisioned a surterranean London of the future where pedestrians would pepper their steps across a network of bridges above the ground, as though walking at street level was a Victorian idea and we should be walking in the air if we ever wanted to progress into the 21st Century. An unfinished bridge within the Barbican that leads to nowhere reveals the result of this unrealised ideal. This is why the Barbican has so many exits and entrances on the roof.

I passed a huge staircase that had been intended to lead into the art gallery but when the designers realised that no one could actually find it they moved the gallery but refused to remove the 'art gallery' sign that had been placed there in anticipation, a perfect indication of the confused nature of this labyrinthine structure. And up above me I saw a shadow moving. And when it stopped and saw me, it started to move more quickly. What I couldn't work out was whether it was heading towards or away from me. The bridge led away but I wouldn't have been surprised if it somehow looped back towards me.

Perhaps foolishly I decided that he was running scared and, feeling a surge of bravery swell within me, tried to find steps that would get me up to his level. I hurried through archways and up stairs but when I was up, where he had been, there was no one there. I continued on, turning several corners until I came to a long passageway. On one side doors were dotted; on the other a barrier overlooked the garden. And at the very end of the passageway, the shape of a figure could be traced. The shadow was darker than before but every second or so it flashed. I soon realised this was the result of the lamps dotted all the way along the passage and also realised that the shadow was getting bigger, heading towards me at an incredible speed, the rapid slap of its footsteps echoing around me.

And in a split second the pursuer who had become the pursued was now the pursuer again. Any sense of bravery I might have had dissolved into the cowardice that rushed beneath it. And I ran, already out of breath from the slightly speedy walking I'd been doing so it didn't take much actual running before exhaustion slammed into my body with such speed that my legs almost buckled.

But it was only fear that kept me moving. And this was when the Barbican really started to betray me. Its confused concrete construction might certainly work against you when you're trying to make it to a play but when you're running for your life, its absurd directionlessness is pretty fucking annoying. There were so many dark crevices, so many miles of subterranean engine rooms, that my beaten, bullet-punctured body could lie undiscovered for years.

My flabby little legs did their very best to get themselves and the rest of me out of danger. They took me up stairs, around corners, along passages, until I found myself on the roof. When I turned back there was nothing at all, not even the echo of footsteps rising from below. I found an open door to a residential stairwell at the base of one of the towers and ran up as far as I could. I hid in a cleaning cupboard and stood there terrified amongst the mops and brooms until a cleaning lady found me the next morning and screamed. There I was, mop in hand, ready to strike. Naturally that was my cue to run away, to head out blinking wildly into the morning light. It was only once I sat down on the tube that I realised that the mop was still in my hand.

Chapter AF

When I got back to my flat the phone was ringing. It was a voice I hadn't heard in a long while.

'Eugene,' said a quiet voice.

'Melissa! Where have you been? Are you okay?'

'I'm scared.'

'Scared?'

'He's back…'

'Who's back?'

'I don't know how but David's back.'

'You've *seen* him?'

'I think I have. He's been leaving me notes and I'm sure it was him who was following me. I thought I was going mad but then last night I heard his voice. He called me, said he wanted to meet me.'

'But David's dead, you know he is. You put him in the ground.'

'I *know*, Eugene, but he's back from the dead.'

'It must be a hoax. Someone is trying to frighten you.'

'I know David's voice. It *was* him. It's just…'

'Just what?'

'He threatened me. He said if I don't see him tonight then I will regret it.'

'Have you called the police?'

'He said he'd hurt me if I told anyone.'

'Get your stuff and get out of there. Come meet me.'

'No, I can't. He'll find me. Whatever I do he'll find me.'

'Listen, where are you going to meet him?'

'He's given me directions.'

'I'll come with you.'

'No, I have to go alone. But you could follow me.'

'Follow you?'

'For protection, to make sure nothing happens to me.'

'Where shall I meet you?'

She named a service station on the A40. She said she'd be there at eight o'clock.

Chapter AG

Her eyes appeared in the crack of the door. The instant she saw me she slammed it shut again.

'Go away!'

'Please, Charlotte, I need to talk to you.'

'Go away, please.'

'I won't take up much time. I have to talk to you about David.'

'I never want to hear that name again.'

'I know you're not going to believe me but David's back.'

There was silence. Those eyes appeared again.

A tarantula sat dormant in a tank.

'Don't tap on the glass,' she said. 'He doesn't like it. That's Charlie the spider, the only male in my life. I love his philosophy. He just takes it easy, the calmest creature in the world. He's also incredibly gentle. Wouldn't harm a fly.' I walked over to the next tank where a chameleon was smiling up at me.

'You certainly have a thing for cold-blooded animals.'

'Would you like to hold Charlie?'

'Oh no, that's quite all right,' I said. She was already

lifting the lid on the tank and reaching in. Before I knew it she was lowering Charlie onto my hand. And the moment those eight legs touched my palm fear turned to calm. He didn't seem to move a muscle and his still nature appeared to transfer through to me. He was very soft and I observed his intricate body. I tried to look him in the eye but there were eight to choose from.

'I had the strangest call from Melissa,' I said, watching the spider. 'She said that David called her.'

Charlotte sighed. 'I don't know anything anymore. I can't say that it's the strangest thing that has happened recently.'

'No?'

'What I found strange is that I had to find out about David's funeral *after* it was all over. Why didn't Melissa tell the hospital?'

'I have no idea.'

'I don't want anything to do with this anymore. The last few weeks have been truly horrific for me. I feel completely destroyed and have not been able to function. But I think Melissa really is going mad. She must be having a hard time differentiating between fantasy and reality. She's made all this up in her head and she's trying to drag you back into it.'

My eyes were following a bank of photographs that had been pinned to a noticeboard. There were parents, brothers, sisters, cousins.

'There he is,' said Charlotte pointing. And out of all these faces David's emerged. 'That was from an office dinner we had once.' There were a few other people in the photo with him.

'Who's this?' I asked.

'Who?'

'The redhead.'

'That's Melissa, of course.'

'Oh yeah.' I looked closer. Much closer. 'How stupid of me.'

Chapter AH

I pulled into the car park of the service station. At the unlit end a single car had been parked and inside I could just about make out the outline of Melissa. I stayed back, turned off my engine and flashed my lights. I stepped out of the car, one foot on the asphalt, only to see her lights flick back on and her engine fire up. Her car spun around and raced towards the exit. I jumped back into my car, fired up the engine and only caught up with her as she slid onto the motorway, my stare fixed on those eyes in her rearview mirror. They never once looked back at me.

Her car floated on into the night and miles passed, the traffic thinning out until there were only two lone cars humming along the winding tarmac. She kept to the fast lane, going as quickly as she could. I pushed my car to its limits in an attempt to keep up with her, following those twin tail lights with determination, keeping my sights locked on them. My lack of understanding as to where we were going, and the tense grip I held on the steering wheel, turned the journey into a torturous feat of endurance. We raced so far that the lights that lit the motorway disappeared, leaving only the beams of our headlights to guide us. I kept my eye on the petrol gauge; I had no idea we would be going such a distance and I feared that needle would soon be travelling through the red.

Her tail lights disappeared and my eyes dotted around to relocate them. I hit a hard left, turning off the motorway down a near-invisible road. We were now firmly in the countryside and London was a distant memory. Those red tail lights lifted and dipped as the road ahead of us unwound itself. It was as though we had found our own little patch of the world that was entirely uninhabited, rushing through thick forest, black-brown trees and dying foliage.

Those two tail lights disappeared again and as I approached I saw that she had turned through an iron gate. Ahead of me stretched a long path which I rolled along, the gravel crunching under me. I could see the moon throwing its light over the trees across the field. The path continued and out of the beams of my headlights grew a large solitary house.

Her car was parked and the front door of the house was open. In the driveway Melissa's car flickered to darkness. The front door was open and a man stood out in the cold, his eyes on me.

I stopped, let my engine run. He approached me and pointed to a space in the driveway. I pulled over and in my rearview mirror I saw Melissa getting out of her car. He spoke to her, exchanged a few words. I turned off the engine, switched off the lights. Melissa was now standing in the driveway too. In the corner I could see a pristine silver Mercedes glinting in the moonlight.

I opened my door and let one foot crunch down on the gravel and then the other. The man walked quickly towards me. He was wearing an apron over a thick jumper. A smile drew itself across his face.

'I hope your journey wasn't too bad,' he said, holding his hand out to me. 'I'm so glad to finally meet you.' I shook his hand.

'Who are you?' I asked.

'Don't you know who I am? I'm David.'

Chapter AI

My eyes raced to take in the details of his hair, face and clothes. It felt far too eerie to be so close to this mythical figure who had obsessed me, haunted me, who had disappeared off the face of the Earth. He didn't look like he did in his photograph. He was older, his hair thinning on top and grey at the temples. He was rounder in the middle than I had been expecting and his voice did not fit the face in that image I carried around.

From the driveway he had quickly taken me to the wine cellar to select a bottle. It seemed to be a matter of urgency for him.

'Merlots, Cabernets, Malbecs... After all the trouble we have caused you it is only fair that I allow you to choose.' He pulled a bottle out and read the label. 'The Douro Valley, Portugal. We spent two weeks there last summer. Sound okay to you?'

'Fine,' I said.

'Good, good. We want to be nothing if not hospitable. Melissa will have the dinner ready soon.'

'Dinner?'

'You don't expect us to drink this on an empty stomach, do you? It's late and you must be hungry.' I *was* starving - but that was not the point. 'You like sausages? I went out this morning and got the best from the local farmer.' My instincts were telling me to make my excuses and go but those sausages did sounds good. 'After dinner I will have to show you my collection of antique firearms. I'm quite the history buff.'

When we headed up to the kitchen the smell hit me and now even my feet were convinced.

He took me into the living room.

'Take a seat, please. You must be tired from your journey. Are you much of a Scotch drinker?'

'Not really.'

'That's disappointing. I thought it was mother's milk to you detectives.' He slapped me hard on the back and laughed heartily, turning red from his own joke. 'You'll like this stuff though,' he said, pouring a couple of glasses from a decanter. He clinked a trio of ice cubes into the glass and handed it over. 'It's from Japan. Years ago the Japanese went to Scotland, learnt everything they needed to, went back home and got to making some of the very best whisky in the world. They are very good at taking something and perfecting it. Pretty soon they'll be overtaking the Scots and winning all the prizes.' That was all very well but I couldn't stand the stuff. He sat opposite me. 'Just take gentle sips. Don't rush it.' I did as he said but still didn't like it. 'What notes do you get? I get…' he said, sticking his nose in the glass and then sipping the tiniest drop. 'Oakiness, nutmeg… almost cinnamon.' I didn't get any of that. I just got the sensation of booze burning in my throat.

The room around us was filled with books.

'These all yours?' I asked.

'I've read every single one of the books in here. I just hoover these things up. Mostly it's medical books, academic books. They can get pretty dry. But I like fiction for entertainment.'

'I can see you read a lot of crime.' Rows of cheap detective novels lined the shelves.

'Oh yes, I'm absolutely addicted to those. I can't get enough of them. I always like to figure out whodunnit, like to challenge myself, to see if I can work it out by the final page. My record is chapter two. I even tried to write one myself but it turned out too knotty. Not that I don't come up with ideas all the time. I've got a drawer full of them.'

'Did you write your own story?' He laughed but it seemed out of place.

'Oh, that's a good one. How do you like it so far?'

'Not so convincing.'

'Well, that's the problem I had. How do you make it *convincing*? I thought it's been pretty convincing so far. How do you feel you've played your part?'

'How do you mean?'

'Oh, come on,' he said laughing, a big grin on his face. 'You've done an admirable job playing a detective but you can't expect anyone to actually be convinced you really are a sleuth. There is no authenticity to your performance. It's paper thin. Look at your costume, for one. I mean, a raincoat, *really*? That's the biggest cliché in the book.'

'Well if I played the part of a detective, what part did you play?'

'Mastermind.'

'Mastermind?'

'You can't say you haven't been impressed.'

'Why would I be impressed?'

'You haven't worked it all out yet, have you? I know it's quite a brainteaser.'

'I'm less interested in the question of how you did it and far more interested in why.'

He laughed again. 'Then you're far further behind than I thought.'

'It's ready!' called Melissa from the other room.

'You shall have to hold that thought,' he said as he picked up his drink and gestured me into the kitchen.

The kitchen table had been laid and I took my seat.

'You must think this all rather strange,' said Melissa, bringing the gravy boat over from the Aga and pouring it liberally over the chubby sausages sitting atop a mashed potato mountain, 'but we appreciate your work.' 'We both do,' added David. 'I was just telling Eugene that we get these sausages from a local farmer.'

'We get all kinds from him. Steak, eggs, sausages. You should try their bacon.'

'Do you like bacon?'

'Of course I do.'

'Do we have any sausages left?' he asked Melissa.

'There's lots more.'

'Then that settles it. Tomorrow morning you will have eggs, sausage and bacon. The best you've ever had.'

I sliced a sausage and shoved it in my mouth before speaking.

'In the morning? I'm not staying.'

'Where do you expect to go? It's so late,' he said.

'You can sleep in the spare room.'

'Tonight you're our guest. Just relax.'

My mouth was full of meaty sausage and creamy mash.

'These are really good.'

'Told you so. More wine?' he asked.

It wasn't a question that required an answer since my glass was already being filled up. David and Melissa's plates were empty.

'Are you not having any?'

'I'm afraid I'm pescatarian,' he said.

'Pescatarian?'

'Ever since I became a doctor.'

'Then how come you have all these sausages?'

'They're for you.'

I laughed a little. 'But... you didn't know... I was coming.' The food itself was too good to resist so I just kept shovelling it into my mouth.

I shut my eyes momentarily and opened them again. 'I mean, this is *really* good but what I don't understand is...' I trailed off.

'What don't you understand?' asked David.

'You...' I said, waving my knife at David, 'you're supposed to be... and you...,' I said, waving my knife at Melissa, 'you're supposed to be...' A cloud of fatigue settled over me.

'Where's my money?' asked David. I didn't really hear him.

'This is *delicious*...' I said, deliriously.

'Where's my money?' David asked again.

I stopped eating to sway a little in my chair.

'Excuse me,' I said, rising from the table. 'Thank you for dinner but I think I'm going to go now.' I pushed my chair away, took one step, and swiftly collapsed onto the floor.

Chapter AJ

Floral wallpaper and children's toys. My eyes absorbed the room. When I tried to move I discovered that my hands were bound together and attached by a single length of rope to the iron headboard. I sat up on the bed and set my feet on the carpet. The rope that bound me was a thick, brown, dusty old thing that burned my skin. I sidled up to the headboard and sunk the rope between my teeth, gnawing at the monstrous knot but nothing I could do would release me.

I stood up, a fat man attached to a bed. I could see through the window that looked out onto the misty field and the cloudy trees beyond. Listening carefully all I could hear was early birdsong but nothing from inside the house. The colour of the light suggested that it was early morning.

I pulled the rope tight, the bed creaking as I put all my weight into dragging it a few inches along the floor. I forced it another few inches, then another. With every inch I moved closer to the door, not that I could turn the knob once I got there. The bolt was clearly present between the lock and the frame and the only view the keyhole offered was a misty darkness.

I looked around for something to cut the rope with. On top of the dresser, alongside a row of My Little Ponies, was a hair brush, a comb and a pair of knitting needles. I cautiously picked up one of the the needles, returned to the bed and jammed the needle into the knot on the bedhead.

The knot started to loosen. I gnawed again, felt it coming loose and soon it fell away. Now I just had to untie the rope around my wrists. I grabbed the door handle. The knob was more likely to come off long before I would be able to force it open.

But then I heard footsteps. I pushed the bed back, flung the rope over the headboard and jumped on. My senses were heightened as I listened to the sound of a lock turning. The door opened and I closed my eyes.

The door shut. Someone was in the room with me.

'Eugene,' whispered a voice.

My eyes flashed open to see Melissa standing in front of the door in her nightgown. She hurried to me.

'I came to check on you.'

'Melissa, you have to let me go!'

'I can't. It's just not possible.'

'Untie me!'

'It's not me. It's David. He says I have no choice. We have no choice.'

'*You* have a choice. I'll be out of here in no time and you'll never hear from me again, I swear it. Melissa, you have to help me.'

I looked into her eyes and saw my own terror reflected back at me.

'You don't understand. You don't understand how deep he's gone, the horror I've seen. You don't understand what he'd do to me. It's the money, you see, the money that's changed him.'

'I don't know anything about the money.'

'He said it would be easy, promised me it would all go okay but nothing's okay. It's all gone so horribly wrong.'

'Melissa…' She wasn't listening. 'I have nothing to do with this. You have to let me go.'

'Oh but you have everything to do with it. You were part of the plan.'

'The plan?' She headed for the door.

'Carly.' She stopped, turned. 'Let me go. I know everything. You'll never get away with it.' The door opened and David grabbed her.

'What the hell do you think you're doing?'

'We have to help him, David. We have to let him go.'

'Get out of here!' He pushed her out of the door and slammed it behind her, leaving me alone with him. He looked like he'd just been woken from sleep. He was still wearing his pyjamas and his hair was all over the place.

'What are we going to do with you?' he asked.

'You can let me go, that's what you can do with me.'

'Oh we can't do that now. You know far too much.' He sighed, pulled up a chair. 'Tell me, what is it about me that obsesses you so much? Melissa told you to stop looking yet you carried on, couldn't help sticking your nose in even after you had been told to disappear. You're not even a real detective.'

'You're not even really dead.'

'I am dead. Technically, that is. On the record, I don't exist. It would be pretty hard for me to get a library card these days.'

'If you're standing here then who did they pull out of

the lake?'

'No idea. We only borrowed him. He was quickly replaced. It's just that he was tagged with my name when he was put back.'

'Who was he?'

'I forget his name. Simon... Steven... Something like that.'

'You *buried* him.'

'Yes, we did. A very tasteful send off, don't you think? I think his family would have been proud.'

'How could you?'

'The man was already dead. You couldn't have saved him. What's the difference if he gets buried in one place or another? The worms would have got him soon enough wherever he was buried. At least he got a good Christian burial. It's what he would have wanted. Or maybe not. I have no idea. But you saw him being sent off, lowered into the ground. I'm sure you thought that it was a fine funeral. I certainly found it very tasteful.'

'You were there?'

'I wouldn't have missed it for the world. I would recommend attending your own funeral if you ever get a chance. You have the opportunity to hear others talk about you unimpeded by your presence. The things you hear about yourself are just fascinating. I was really rather appreciated while I was alive. Shame I'm now in the underworld.

'I was so impressed with Melissa. The whole thing was just so convincing. Melissa became someone new altogether, wrote that entire eulogy all by herself and memorised it too. From the beginning she's been note-perfect. But you know you were probably sucked in more than anyone. You bought the whole thing from the very start. That hook really pierced right through your cheek. I watched you wandering the streets. You had no idea what you were doing, just wandering aimlessly from one place to another. I was there when you first came to the house. I watched you coming from the window upstairs and I thought you were just perfect. You looked like such an idiot in that raincoat of yours. I listened to the whole meeting downstairs, heard every word. We didn't think you'd cause us any trouble. And later I'd watch you walking around in your own little world, oblivious to what was around you, oblivious that the man you were looking for was right behind you. I could even cross your path and you wouldn't see me. I mean you're a pretty terrible detective. If this really was a matter of life and death any real client would have asked for their money back by now.'

'Why did you even involve me in the first place?'

'You added that extra level of authenticity. If Melissa hired a private detective to look for me then no one could claim that she wasn't *really* looking for me. You see we couldn't hire a good private detective in case they actually started to suspect what was going on. No, we needed a detective who could be easily fooled, a bumbling idiot, you could say. When we found your ad online I thought it was too good to be true. "Private Detective For Hire. No Case Too Small." You were our witness for hire. I honestly never thought you would take it so seriously. You really thought you were onto something. And then you went too far, needled away, became a real nuisance. And we were so close. Everyone was convinced that I was gone for good and the payout was almost ours. And then that insurance inspector John Jones tells Melissa that he is going to be speaking to you, just to clear up a few loose ends. Then as soon as he interviews you he withdraws payment. What on Earth did you tell him?'

'He didn't buy your story from the start.'

'He told us the money was as good as ours.'

'You really have a very loose grip on reality, don't you? There's no kind of fraud that he hasn't seen before. A case comes in where a man has taken out life insurance and is found dead not long after that. That file might as well have had a big flashing red light attached. Not only that but *suicide*. They don't pay out for suicide. Read the contract.'

'They *do* pay out for suicide as long as it's committed after twelve months after signing.'

'So you waited an extra couple of months? So what? There is nothing I could have said to convince him. He had already made his mind up by the time he met me.'

'You don't know how much work I put into planning this. I read everything I could find, checked and double checked. I could tell you every case of life insurance fraud of the 20th Century. I've seen every movie where they try to pull it off, read every book, but everyone who fails has something in common. They don't think it through and eventually something trips them up. This plan was beautiful, a work of art on paper. Unfortunately for me I tripped over a fat detective.'

'You were doomed from the start.'

'I was doomed from the moment that you entered the picture. I wish we'd never had the misfortune of meeting.'

'The feeling's mutual.'

'Where did you learn to play poker?'

'I don't know how to play poker.'

'You hustled pretty good.'

'Hustled?'

'Pretending you had no idea and then clearing the table? From what I heard it was pretty remarkable. There's only one problem.'

'What's that?'

'You were playing with my money. It means that everything you won actually belongs to me. And not only that but you stole my identity, took my name. What have you done with my money?'

'Your money? You're insane.'

'That may be the case but I want my winnings.'

'I don't have the winnings.'

'Just think about me for a moment. Because of you I have been left not only without a penny to my name but also without the name itself. You have completely wiped out my name, deleted me from the history books. So the least you could do is give me what is rightfully mine.'

'I don't have your money.'

'Don't say that to me again.' He approached the bed and as he did so his hand reached for the rope. He pulled it and was surprised to find it hanging loose in his hand. I used this as my opportunity to spring up from the bed and plough into David, slamming him against the wardrobe. I grabbed the door handle and swung the door open. About to run out, David grabbed the rope and jerked me back into the room. I ran back against him, smashing my head into his. I think it did more pain to me than it did to him but it at least got that rope out of his hands and allowed me to run out the door and tumble down the stairs.

Chapter AK

My foggy brain understood that I was running for my life, my legs locked in desperate repetition, my hands still bound behind my back. The Earth rushed beneath me as the foliage crunched beneath my battered leather shoes. I was deep within the forest behind the house. Away behind me I could hear David's voice shouting out. I was too occupied with the mechanics of running to take notice, my brain telling my legs to put one foot in front of the other as quickly as they could. The assumption had been made that through the simple act of running I could live another hour.

The trees cleared and I found myself at an opening. My feet were suddenly wet right up to the ankle. I looked down to find my feet in a thick boggy soup that stretched out in front of me.

I heard rustling in the distance. I stepped further out into the bog until my knees were submerged, then my waist, then my stomach. As I saw a disturbance in the trees from where I had come from, I ducked down, submerging my whole body to my neck. My raincoat expanded in the black sludge around me and I dragged it down under the surface.

From where I was I could see David hit the water too.

His head darted around, astonished that I had disappeared into thin air.

He stepped around the perimeter of the bog, approaching the bushes where I was hiding.

'Where the hell are you?' he asked into the trees. I held my breath.

I lowered myself further until my chin dipped into the freezing black goop. I was determined not to move from my place, not to cause any noticeable ripples in the bog that would lead David to me.

But even after David had headed back into the forest, I remained there for a good while to make sure that he wouldn't return. As I rose from the liquid what emerged was a tar-black figure. From my neck down, all through my raincoat and my clothes and shoes, that thick, boggy mud had taken over me. The fabric clung to my body, all inky black and cold. It added extra weight and every step became an additional effort. I limped off as far as I could.

I found a tree with jagged bark and started to scrape the rope that bound my wrists together against it. As the morning turned to full colour around me the thick mud started to dry and harden. I could feel it tightening my skin but also stiffening my clothes, creating a kind of crust around my body. It made moving with any great speed very difficult but once that rope fell to the dirt I forced myself to push on, just making sure I kept moving.

The forest didn't seem to end. It was so thick and so dark that it felt as though all I was doing was pushing deeper into it.

I became too exhausted to continue on so I sat down and leaned against a tree. Allowing myself to stop moving, to listen to the peacefulness around me, caused the grip of fear to loosen momentarily. And this allowed my whole body fell into the deepest sleep.

I was awoken by violent shivers. The bare, wiry branches of the towering trees that surrounded me crisscrossed the clouds above. They had turned metallic, twisting fiercely together.

I got myself onto my feet and kept walking. The more I walked the more the forest wrapped itself around me and I realised it was never-ending. I walked for one hour, then two, then three. By the fourth hour every part of me burned. The sky had darkened and I was forced to walk with my arms outstretched.

The fear had not dissipated since that morning, it was just my concerns that had changed. I didn't know if I would ever get out of there, if I would freeze to death in the middle of this pitch-black forest. And then it appeared, that light in the distance, glinting amidst the branches. It was an opening, a sign of escape, a final way out of this nightmare.

But when I reached the opening I wished that the bog had swallowed me up. What I was looking at was the very house I had escaped from. I had found the only entrance into this woody labyrinth and it seemed like I had now found the only way out. How all those hours were wasted I could not understand.

I was hoping that my muddy appearance would help camouflage me under the shadow of night, but more likely it was all too easy to spot the fat man moving across the landscape if you were only to look. I slipped onto my back and travelled along the wet, grassy earth. I picked myself up and crept towards the house. I could hear raised voices inside, an argument in full swing, but I couldn't make out any discernible words.

I clambered over a small wall, inelegantly falling to the gravel and darting towards my car. The burglar light flashed on and suddenly I was in full view, my key scrabbling for the lock. I heard the front door open behind me and when I turned my face managed to catch a cricket bat mid-swing.

Chapter AL

Within my skull a buzzing emerged, a low, sustained note that rang through me. My eyes opened just a slit and let a fog pour in. A cracked, pulsating pain hit me from inside my face and spread out in all directions. The blood everywhere told me that this was no nosebleed.

Through the fog a dimly lit room outlined itself. Boxes everywhere, sacks of charcoal, cans of paint. Along one wall lay those bottles of wine.

The shadow of David White emerged out of the darkness.

I was tied to a chair, my arms bound behind me again. I struggled but the intricate knots of the rope kept my limbs firmly entwined with the limbs of the chair.

'I had to get more rope, you know, to make it all the way around you.'

My jaw quickly let me know that talking was going to be painful. 'Sorry for the inconvenience,' I said.

He walked over to a wall and unhooked a reel of cable. He ran it through his hands a few times before raising a length of it above his head.

'Where is it?' he asked.

He whipped my face, burning a line across my forehead, my nose and my cheek.

'Where is what?' I screamed. He struck me harder this time, putting all his strength into it, inflicting as much pain as he possibly could. It felt like it was slicing straight through me. He struck me repeatedly, indiscriminately, hitting my scalp, my face, my neck, my shoulders. Rather than screams all that emerged from me were tortured, elongated moans.

'Where is my money?'

'I don't have it.' He sliced through me again.

'Say it again.'

'I don't have it.' Another.

'You spent my money?' I could hardly speak.

'I didn't mean to win it.'

'What's all this about you never playing poker before?'

'I didn't know what I was doing, I swear.'

'I don't believe you.'

'It was beginner's luck.'

'Luck... I don't believe in it.' He raised his arm again.

'I know about Carly,' I said.

'What?'

'Carly.' He seemed to grow quiet.

'What do you know?'

'That Melissa's Carly, that Carly's Melissa. I know everything.'

That cable came down upon me with such violence that it seemed to knock me out of this world. The pain engulfed me, took me over until it was all I knew. I couldn't feel anything else anymore and I didn't know who I was or what had happened and I had no idea when he left because when I came to the room was dark and empty and my body burned and what had happened echoed like a terrifying dream.

In the darkness that buzzing returned, that torturous buzzing that seeped through my bones and into my brain. I rattled in that chair, kicked my legs, twisted my arms but I couldn't move.

I don't know if you have ever been incarcerated before but it really gives you a lot of time to think. I mean, what else is there to do? Your brain goes into overdrive, starts recalling things you haven't thought about for years and with such conviction that it really takes you back to another place and time. I thought about my little sister and my mother and my father and how I hadn't seen them in so long. And I thought about my grandmother. And I thought about the girl I used to be in love with. And out of nowhere, from just the most superficial thought of them, just from the thought that they existed, I started to weep like a little boy. It had hit me that I was a terrible brother and son. The fact that my family never entered my thoughts just proved that. And I felt immense sorrow swell inside of me and all I wanted to do was reach out to them. But I've always felt that tears are essentially selfish, that one cries because they are crying for themselves. It is a selfish act, and so it was in this case. I was crying for myself out of self-pity and crying for the fact that I might never see them again.

And I was back at my office desk, staring out of the window at that concrete car park, recalling that sensation of suffocation and my hands shackled to that desk. But I felt so foolish. There are millions of people out there who have to take a boring commute, who are forced to do a job they don't like. Why should I be so special as to demand adventure out of life? Sitting down there in that freezing basement I absolutely longed to be back at that desk. I longed for a signal failure on that commute amidst all those strangers, longed for the faces and incessant small talk of my colleagues and above all I longed for that intense sense of boredom. I would be *thrilled* by boredom. I wanted the luxury to be bored, to have enough time to be bored. And as my tears subsided my nose began to streak red down my face and onto my shirt. I just sat and watched the steady drip, drip, drip, like a tap in need of tightening, as it coloured the fabric.

I managed to hop. I'll say that again: I managed to hop. With the right kind of bodily jerk I managed to lift the chair millimetres from the ground. I did it again, then again, jumping barely into the air, moving a fraction at a time. My eye was on the tools scattered on a nearby work bench but I never made it that far. The wooden chair split apart under me, just collapsed into pieces. I squirmed around on the floor and managed to wriggle free from the rope and wood.

I ran up the stairs and grabbed the handle. Locked.

I fetched a hammer to smash the lock off but I was stopped in my tracks by that buzzing which was now louder than ever. The door to an adjacent room was ajar and I pushed it open to find a light emanating from a machine at the back, a whirring monster of a machine. As I approached it revealed itself to be a large stand-alone refrigerator. I lifted the lid to find that it was full to the brim with ice but discoloured ice, red in some places. I ran the hammer through the red cubes only to find human fingers underneath. The fingers, rigid and frozen, were connected to a hand which was connected to an arm. I didn't know that David was already in the room with me.

'Get away from there.'

I span around to find him standing in the doorway, a pistol in his hand. He raised it to my face and squeezed the trigger. No bang, no blast, no bullet out of that bony little gun. He looked lost, confused as to why the little weapon had not done the only thing it was designed to do. He threw it at me but it hit the wall behind me. I leapt right at him and sent the hammerhead crashing into his skull.

I ran up the stairs, out of the basement, and straight for the front door. My hand was on the handle when the frosted glass exploded and fragments shot out in every direction. Behind me was Melissa standing in the hallway, eyes closed, a smoking double-barrelled antique gun in her hand.

When she opened her eyes they were filled with fear.

'What have you done to him?' she asked, trembling.

'Put the gun down and we can talk.'

'No, Eugene. It has to end here.'

'Do you even know how to use that thing?'

'You just point and shoot.'

'But you've got the safety on.'

For a brief second she checked and it gave me the chance to swipe my hand at the barrel. Just for the record, I don't know a single thing about guns. I have no idea if a double-barrelled shotgun has a safety or not. I managed to get a grip on it but she ripped it from me and it went flying to the floor.

I turned to run but Melissa launched at me, grabbing and kicking as viciously as she could. I tried to grab her arms, to grab anything, but my hand got caught up in her hair. I tangled strands of it in my fist and when I pulled that beautiful red hair slipped off so easily, revealing a scalp of brown hair underneath. She transformed before me from one person into another.

This didn't stop her from fighting and I had to use all my force to get myself out of that door and into the driveway. I knew she'd gone for the gun as I unlocked my car.

But it wasn't Melissa who came out of the house, it was David, his face saturated with blood, shotgun in hand. He was aiming as my wheels spun on the gravel and the car sped into motion. As I tore through the gate my back windscreen exploded and let the cold night air rush in.

Far down the road headlights appeared in the rearview mirror. A second glance revealed that the car was now much closer. If I hadn't sped up as fast as that little hatchback could manage, he would most certainly have hit me. I was now forced to hastily negotiate the road and all those trees that were rushing past me. When a bend appeared it almost sent me flying off into a ditch but I managed to keep the tyres on the tarmac.

A chase ensued and while my speedometer was at eighty-five, this little car was no real match for the monster in my rearview mirror. It rammed into me, forcing me to momentarily lose control and then tighten my grip on the steering wheel. There was no way I would be able to hold out much longer. I needed an escape and my eyes darted around the beam of my headlights. A little way ahead I saw my chance and a sudden turn of the wheel, a sharp 90-degrees, allowed me to spin off onto another road. My pursuer was forced to brake suddenly and receded into the distance in my mirror.

I shut my headlights off and refrained from braking. I didn't want those tail lights to give me away. The road ahead and the woodland around me disappeared and now I really was plunged into darkness, the moonlight offering the merest outline of surfaces. I could only just make out the road ahead of me. The car flew along with such speed that it felt like it was gliding through the air but it wasn't long before those headlights appeared behind me, illuminating the road ahead. It was gaining on me quickly, my foot pushed down as far as it could go. At that moment the engine behind me screamed and the car launched right into the back of me and I could feel the crunch of metal. My car jolted but I gripped the wheel so tightly that I managed to keep it steady. That engine roared again and at that moment I experienced the most violent collision you could imagine. It knocked my mind out of my body, sent me flying into the air and spun the world into a tight knot. My life did not flash before my eyes but instead I marvelled at how the car had taken flight like this and for a brief moment the only question I had was how did I ever get into this mess? And then I experienced a darkness so black that it could more accurately be described as nothing at all.

Chapter AM

The spectre was sitting beside my hospital bed, still as can be, her gloved hands clasped firmly in her lap. She hadn't removed her dark green herringbone overcoat and scarlet red cloche hat.

She filled the room's silence with words.

'We wouldn't have to work again, he told me. I was caught under a spell, just totally under his control. I was saturated with love for him and could think of nothing else. No one had ever paid me so much attention before. He lavished gifts on me, placed me at the centre of his world. We met during my first week at the hospital but the infatuation took time to take hold. Working late one night he asked if I'd go to dinner with him. I didn't have anything else on so I agreed and was surprised when he took me to this really fancy restaurant. It was only over dinner that he told me he was married. He told me as though it was no big deal, as though it was something I should just accept. He produced a small box containing two diamond earrings. He told me right there and then that they were Melissa's but he wanted me to wear them. From the very beginning he was very honest about the situation with Melissa, how she was threatening to leave him, how they weren't sleeping in the same bed and just how unhappy they were. I left that evening promising myself that I would not see him outside of work but I knew deep down that it was a promise I would struggle to keep.

'I held off for as long as I could but every time we were left alone another gift would be produced. Bracelets, rings, necklaces, each one another possession of Melissa's. I didn't want to accept them at first but he was insistent. When I put them on he cried, said I reminded him of Melissa in happier times. Only later did I suspect he was making me in her image.

'And I held off taking it any further outside of accepting these gifts. Of course it was very flattering to receive such fine things. But when that barrier broke, when I finally gave into him, it was an absolute explosion of passion. We couldn't keep our hands off each other. We professed our love almost instantly, became giddy teenagers lost in the throes of infatuation. My whole being was taken over by him.

'He told me he was going to leave Melissa. She had wanted to stay in their country house for the weekend and I really didn't want him to go. I was jealous of any moment she spent with him, of any moment she stole from me. But he promised that he would tell her everything and that he would end it all with her. And when I saw him on the Monday he told me that it was all over but it was Melissa who had ended it. She had packed her bags and walked out on him. It was that night that David got down on one knee and presented the ring to me. Even the diamond ring was Melissa's but it fit me so perfectly. It was as though her finger was a mere diversion on the ring's journey to me.

'It was only then that he told me about the trouble he

was in, the debt that had poisoned his relationship with Melissa. I was really worried for him and wanted to do everything I could do to help. He told me how poker used to be something he'd win big on but he had been playing these high stakes games and was in the midst of a deadly losing streak. One morning he arrived at work with a black eye after some guy came over demanding money. They said they'd kill him if he didn't pay. He was at least a hundred thousand pounds in debt.

'That night he drove me to the house of a costumier who had created this auburn wig by hand, hair by hair. She fitted it to me and I was transformed. I was already wearing Melissa's coat, necklace and earrings and this was the final jigsaw piece that completed me in her image.

'He'd planned out exactly how it was all going to work but it was more straightforward in the beginning. He was just going to disappear, look like he had dropped off the face of the Earth. He taught me how to sign Melissa's signature, made me practice it over and over with him. And I sat with him as we signed off the sale of their house. The money helped keep those wolves at bay and in the meantime he knew a friend who was moving to Italy for a few months and asked if he could stay in his place. We moved in together.

'All day and night he would try to figure out just exactly how this could be pulled off. That was when he had the idea of hiring a private detective. It would build my case, prove that I was really looking for him while he was missing. And when we found your ad on the internet it was just perfect. We couldn't believe our luck. He had made sure we found the cheapest detective we could find. If they were too good they could have started to get too close to the truth but when he saw you - he sat at the top of the stairs listening to every word - he was convinced there was no way you could crack it. And when you showed up unannounced one time he had to jump out of the bath and hide in the wardrobe. You opened the very wardrobe he was standing in but for some reason you didn't see him. He was standing right in front of you.

'He got word that you had been gambling under his name and that you'd won the entire pot. He wasn't happy that you had been posing as him and he became determined to get his money back. He felt that any winnings won under his name were rightfully his.

'The more he stayed in the house the more paranoid he got. He thought it would be best if he moved to a hotel and used a completely new identity there but I just couldn't stand being apart from him. He had gone from allowing me to wear the wig only when going out to having to wear it all the time. I even started wearing it when we made love; catching myself in the mirror it looked like he was with someone else entirely.

'He really couldn't sleep. He was becoming unsure of himself, convinced that he had to take it further otherwise the whole plot would have come to nothing. He became convinced that there had to be a body. I didn't like the idea at first but he knew someone who could arrange it. He paid a considerable amount of money to get a body from the morgue and into the boot of his car. The first time I saw the body myself was at the lake. It was such a horrific sight, all twisted inside that car, the very same model of car that David was in when he died.

'Once the body was found I made a claim on the policy that David had taken out and made arrangements for the funeral. We needed it to be as authentic as possible so David gave me a list of names of people he knew but it was important that none of them had met Melissa before so that they wouldn't break my cover. I called them all, invited them and took my role very seriously. I wrote the eulogy, rehearsing it with David until it was perfect. As the day played out I really did start to feel like I was Melissa. My biggest fear was that Melissa herself would show up. Then there would have been mayhem. But David was certain that wouldn't happen.

'He would follow you, you know, watch you as you wandered around the streets, follow you in his car. He'd tell me what you had been up to, say that you'd been wandering the streets aimlessly. He was troubled to see you at the funeral and later he watched you head into the police station. It was at this point that the insurance company interviewed me. They called me in three times and I told them everything I could to the best of my ability. They told me there wouldn't be any issues with the payout but that they just had to verify a few things with you. David found you in a delivery man's outfit, driving a van around town. He was really confused and he followed you in the Mercedes, wanting to find out exactly when you were being interviewed. And when the payment was withdrawn David was just sick with anger and was determined to get those winnings out of you. It would have been enough for us to at least make a getaway out of the country.

'I didn't know what he was going to do to you when we got you to the house but I was really scared when I saw you tied up like that. When he took you to the basement he said he was going to get that money out of you if it was the last thing he did. I just did not know how you escaped. You hurt him pretty badly but I couldn't stop him following after you. I saw the smashed chair in the basement and the bloody hammer and the pistol. And then the refrigerator. I saw her lying there; I saw me lying there, as dead as can be. I knew that's when I couldn't ever see David again. I got into my car and raced away and that's when I found the flames in the darkness, the silver Mercedes crushed and aflame against the tree. I called for an ambulance and drove as far as I could and now I'm never going to stop running.'

Chapter AN

I retired the raincoat, hung it in my wardrobe and exchanged it for a leather jacket I hadn't worn in years.

This fat detective's broken bones took time to heal. It was three months before I put my feet back down on the ground and six months before I could put one foot in front of the other. I was gifted a newfound sense of recovery once I left the hospital and the world opened up to me. I started to find satisfaction in the simplest things around me: fresh air, expressive trees, the warmth of sun rays.

My colleagues nicknamed me Lucky. Lucky because I was still around to tell the tales of my adventures and Lucky because I found a job waiting for me when I was ready to return. After I had described in detail everything that had happened - my capture and escape, the high speed chase and the concertinaing of the car on impact - management weren't too thrilled to get me back onto the road in one of their vans. They found me an unoccupied desk in the back room of the depot where I could spend my days processing order forms. And the monotony that trickled back into my life thrilled me. I took pride in that little desk of mine, a resolutely solid thing with two drawers too stiff to open.

There was great pleasure to be had in the simplicity of the task at hand, moving unprocessed forms from an in-tray on one side of my desk to an out-tray on the other. I even got to brand them with an inky rubber stamp in between.

The commute was a walk this time. There was no tube involved at all and maybe cutting out public transport is a key to happiness. At my quickest pace I could make it there in thirty and if I took my time it was more like forty-five. And on the walk to work I could watch the sun rise, observe the urban world groan to life, and allow my brain to whir away. I found that every morning I couldn't wait to leave my house and be back at that little desk. I was more motivated than I had ever been in my whole life.

Lying on that hospital bed I lost my appetite somewhere. When I was let back into the wild I just could not see kebab shops and fried chicken restaurants in the same way. It was as though that crash had knocked it right out of me. For the first few months of recovery, at least, I was a reformed man.

That didn't mean that I gave up the Friday night pizza though. My grandmother was too insistent and didn't understand the concept of restraint. Those wagon-wheel size pizzas would still show up early Friday and my grandmother and I would point the armchairs towards the television. We would consume hours of TV like we would consume those pizzas until there was nothing left to watch and nothing left to eat. Not even the crusts were safe from our Friday night appetites. After all the game shows, sitcoms and movies were over, and my grandmother had retreated to bed, I headed back to my room. I listened to the screeches of my modem as it dialled up in its uniquely musical way.

Okay, let's say that the thrill of monotony didn't last, that an inkling of restlessness had crept back into me and my imagination drifted back to the raincoat that hung in the dark of my wardrobe. Let's just say that I had already clicked it into existence and there was nothing I could do about it. Amid requests for second-hand piano lessons and first-hand bicycles, it looked distinctly out of place.

Private Detective For Hire. No Case Too Small.

christianhayes.co.uk